'I shall have to f...
secretary,' Brad...

And one who was willing to be his bed-companion, no doubt, Joanne thought sourly. Hoping to give him as much trouble as possible, she assured him, 'I'm quite sure my sister won't let you down.' Recklessly, she added, 'And if by any chance she can't come, I might even volunteer for the post myself!'

A devilish gleam appeared in Brad's eye. 'I might hold you to that... Have you much experience?'

Loathing both him and the *double entendre*, she gave him a come-hither look and cooed, 'Oh, yes, lots.'

Lee Wilkinson lives with her husband in a three-hundred-year-old stone cottage in a Derbyshire village, which most winters gets cut off by snow. They both enjoy travelling and recently, joining forces with their daughter and son-in-law, spent a year going round the world 'on a shoestring' while their son looked after Kelly, their much loved German Shepherd dog. Her hobbies are reading and gardening and holding impromptu barbecues for her long-suffering family and friends.

Recent titles by the same author:

THE VENETIAN'S PROPOSAL
RYAN'S REVENGE
MARRIAGE ON THE AGENDA
WEDDING ON DEMAND
A VENGEFUL DECEPTION

STAND-IN MISTRESS

BY

LEE WILKINSON

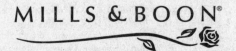

MILLS & BOON®

All the characters in this book have no existence outside the imagination of the author, and have no relation whatsoever to anyone bearing the same name or names. They are not even distantly inspired by any individual known or unknown to the author, and all the incidents are pure invention.

First published in Great Britain 2002
Harlequin Mills & Boon Limited,
Eton House, 18-24 Paradise Road, Richmond, Surrey TW9 1SR

© Lee Wilkinson 2002

ISBN 0 263 82981 2

Set in Times Roman 10½ on 11¼ pt.
01-1102-51790

Printed and bound in Spain
by Litografia Rosés, S.A., Barcelona

CHAPTER ONE

'AND the installation work could be carried out without delay?'

'Yes, certainly.' Cool and efficient-looking in a charcoal-grey suit, her slim, nylon-clad legs neatly crossed, Joanne was quietly confident.

There was a brief pause while the burly managing director of Liam Peters thought it over.

'Well, if your company can give me the kind of service you've just outlined, Miss Winslow, I believe we can do business,' he said pleasantly.

'I'm sure we can,' she promised.

Elbows resting on the arms of his chair, hands steepled, he stared at her across the desk.

Smooth sable hair framed an oval face with good features—dark blue eyes, widely spaced, a generous mouth, a straight nose, and a determined chin.

Not exactly beautiful, he decided, but an interesting face, full of character.

'In that case I'll expect your team of technicians to be here first thing Monday morning to talk to me.'

'They will be,' she assured him, and smiled.

That smile made him revise his previous opinion.

Rising to his feet, he accompanied her to the door of the outer office and they shook hands cordially.

Barely restraining the impulse to jump for joy and shout 'Yippee!' she made her way sedately out of the newly completed office block and into Fulham Road.

She was immediately engulfed by the golden brightness of an early-September afternoon and the ceaseless roar and bustle of London's traffic.

After months of worry, as the economy declined and the company her brother had built up began to founder, things seemed to be looking up.

For over five years Steve had struggled to make Optima Business Services successful, but the recession had meant less work and put a severe strain on the company's slender financial resources.

The first really tricky patch had been weathered by mortgaging their house. But the second squall, coming fast on the heels of the first, had threatened to sink them.

Then, just that morning, Steve had been promised a substantial injection of cash by MBL Finance, an international investment company who specialised in helping small businesses.

Now, heaven be praised, she had as good as secured what promised to be a lucrative contract to set up a large new communications network.

About to head in the direction of the nearest tube station, Joanne glanced at her watch. She was surprised to find it was twenty minutes to five. At this time on a Friday there was no point in going back to their Kensington offices.

She was less than ten minutes' walk away from where they lived, so she might as well go home and start preparing a meal for when the rest of the family got in. Turning, she headed for Carlisle Street, and the house she shared with her brother, Steve, her sister, Milly, and Milly's husband, Duncan.

Milly would no doubt be home by now, packing. The young couple were moving to Scotland, where Duncan, a newly qualified doctor, had recently been offered a position at a practice in his home town of Edinburgh.

A furnished flat above the surgery went with the post, and the journey by overnight sleeper meant they would be in Edinburgh by seven-thirty tomorrow morning, which would allow them plenty of time to get settled in over the weekend.

What had made the offer even more acceptable was that one of the receptionists had recently left, and Milly had been given the chance to take over her job.

Even so, she had seemed edgy and unsettled, less than enthusiastic about moving so far north, and her obvious reluctance had caused some trouble between herself and Duncan.

When she protested, with some passion, that she liked the secretarial job she had now and didn't want to leave, Duncan had pointed out quietly that before she married him he'd made it quite plain that he planned to return to Scotland.

Unable to deny this, she had resorted to tears, and, when they did no good, ragged outbursts of temper. But to Joanne's immense relief, Duncan, as steady and level-headed as Milly was wild and wilful, had largely ignored her tantrums.

When Joanne reached Carlisle Street, which was quiet and tree-shaded, lined by old and elegant town houses with porticoed entrances, she walked down it with her usual feeling of nostalgia.

Number twenty-three had belonged to her parents. A happy family home, its front room had been used as an office, with a gold-lettered sign in the window that read: 'John and Jane Winslow. Solicitors.'

Then five years ago the pair had died together in a train crash in Mexico, while on a second honeymoon.

Milly, the youngest of the family, had been only thirteen at the time. Instead of returning to university for the autumn term, Joanne had joined her brother's business venture so she could be on hand to look after both of them.

Steve had protested that at twenty-two he was old enough to look after himself, but had been only too pleased to have the running of the house taken off his hands.

Joanne climbed the steps, put her key in the lock, and let herself in. She had expected to hear pop music blaring, but the house was still and silent. It seemed Milly wasn't home after all.

When she'd changed from her business suit into trousers and a top, she made her way down to the pleasant, airy kitchen.

Having plugged in the kettle for a cup of tea, and opened up the stove, she began to prepare the evening meal. Lisa, Steve's secretary, and now his fiancée, was coming home with him tonight, so they could make it a family celebration.

With that thought in mind, Joanne found a couple of bottles of sparkling wine and put them in the fridge.

She was in the middle of adding a breadcrumb and pine-kernel topping to the cheese and broccoli bake when Milly appeared in the doorway.

Petite and pretty, with red-gold hair, bright blue eyes and a figure like a pocket Venus, she was usually sparkling and vivacious, dressed up to show off her charms.

Now, wearing scruffy jeans and a shrunken T-shirt, she looked edgy and in low spirits as she slumped down at the table.

'I didn't realise you were home,' Joanne remarked. 'No music.'

'Didn't feel like playing any.'

'Still worrying about the move?' Joanne asked with some sympathy.

When Milly said nothing, she added reassuringly, 'I'm sure there's no need to. Once you've settled in and made some new friends you'll be fine.'

Her face sullen, Milly muttered, 'What about my job? You know how much I enjoy it…'

Rather than go to college, Milly had chosen to take a secretarial course. Quick and intelligent, despite her somewhat flighty ways, she had done well. On completing the course, she had found a job with Lancing International, filling in for one of the secretaries who was on maternity leave.

She had proved so efficient that when the new mother failed to return she had been offered the post on a permanent basis.

'Well, I'm sure you'll find your new job interesting,' Joanne said soothingly.

Milly snorted. 'Depressing, more like. Who wants to be stuck in a doctor's surgery day and night?'

Letting that go, Joanne poured them both a cup of tea and sat down opposite, before enquiring, 'Finished packing?'

'I haven't even started.'

'If you need any help let me know.'

'I'm not sure whether I'm going.' The words were spoken defiantly.

As lightly as possible, Joanne said, 'I don't see you have much choice. All the arrangements are made. And, after all, Duncan is your husband.'

'You don't need to remind me. I wish I'd listened to you when you said I was too young to get married.'

Joanne's heart sank. It was true that, thinking Milly too immature, she had at first opposed the marriage. But Duncan had seemed both sensible and stable, and the pair had been so very much in love, that she had finally given her blessing.

'Duncan and I have quarrelled so much lately that I'm beginning to wonder if the whole thing was a mistake,' Milly added miserably.

Hiding her dismay, Joanne said calmly, 'You know perfectly well that you're only feeling this way because of the move.'

Taking a gulp of her tea, Milly shook her head. 'There's more to it than that.'

'Stuff and nonsense,' Joanne said briskly.

'You don't understand. I think I'm in love.'

'As you've only been married for a few months I should hope so.'

'I don't mean with Duncan. I still care about him, of course, but I think I've fallen for someone else.'

'If it's Trevor, he will be flattered.' Joanne tried to make a joke of it.

Diverted, Milly pulled a face. 'What you see in that pompous git I can't imagine… You may not be Miss World but you could do better than him.'

'Thanks,' Joanne said drily.

'Duncan doesn't rate him either,' Milly added, as though that settled it. 'He has about as much charisma as a worm without any charisma.'

'I certainly wouldn't call Trevor a worm,' Joanne objected mildly.

'Neither would I, on second thoughts. He's too picky and bossy. He'd want to tell you what to do all the time.'

'I'll bear that in mind. I should hate to marry the wrong man.'

'Like me, you mean?'

'Don't be an idiot!' Joanne exclaimed with a sharpness born of fear. 'You haven't married the wrong man. Duncan is exactly what you need.'

'But I keep trying to tell you… I've fallen for someone else.'

Taking a deep breath, Joanne said, 'Well, if it isn't Trevor, you'd better tell me who it is.'

'My boss. Brad Lancing… Now, he *is* charismatic.'

'Brad Lancing!'

'He's absolutely gorgeous! Handsome, clever, and totally charming… He has the most fascinating eyes you've ever seen… And that mouth…' Milly practically drooled.

So that explained Milly's moods, her reluctance to leave her job. Joanne groaned inwardly.

Seeing the look on her sister's face, Milly said, 'You think I'm just being a fool, don't you?'

'According to Steve, Lancing is a married man with children, so the answer's yes.'

'Steve's wrong. I know for a fact that he *isn't* married and he *hasn't* any children. He's a thirty-year-old bachelor.'

Unsure which version to believe, Joanne countered, 'And you're an eighteen-year-old married woman.'

'Age doesn't matter, and I don't feel married when I'm with him. I feel…well…*wonderful*.'

'Oh, Milly,' Joanne said helplessly, 'don't you know that a lot of women fall for their boss, while most bosses scarcely notice their secretary?'

'Brad notices me,' Milly assured her triumphantly. 'The two nights I told you I was working late, I was having dinner with him.'

Suddenly scared half out of her wits, Joanne croaked, 'You didn't go any further?'

'No, I didn't. But from some of the things he said, and the way he looked at me, I know he wanted to.'

Joanne gritted her teeth. When Milly had first started to work for the company, Steve had mentioned that Lancing had a bad reputation as far as women were concerned.

But she hadn't worried, never dreaming that a sophisticated man like him would be even remotely interested in a girl who was just eighteen, and newly married, to boot.

He must be a complete and utter swine, and totally without scruples.

'Surely you realise a man like that is only out for what he can get?' she said desperately. 'And when—'

'Don't tell me, I know… When he's got it he won't respect me. Well, I'm fed up with being *respected*. I want some excitement in my life, and if this trip to Norway does come off…' She stopped speaking abruptly.

'What trip to Norway?'

'If it turns out to be necessary, Brad will be going to Norway for six weeks or so on business. He's asked me to go with him.'

Tight-lipped, Joanne demanded, 'As what?'

'His secretary, of course,' Milly answered demurely.

'But you're no longer working for him. You've given in your notice.'

Milly shook her head. 'I haven't said anything about leaving. I haven't made up my mind about going to Scotland…' Seeing the look on her sister's face, she faltered to a halt.

Joanne's cup rattled into the saucer. 'You can't seriously mean that you're willing to risk destroying your marriage because of a silly infatuation?'

'Oh, but I—'

'Hasn't it occurred to you that Brad Lancing probably only wants a brief fling? Another notch on his bedpost? Even if I'm mistaken about him being married, he has a reputation as a Casanova… And what about your wedding vows?'

'I was too young to tie myself for life.'

'At the time you assured me you were ready for the responsibilities of marriage.'

'Well, I thought I was.'

'So did I. And so did Duncan. But if you're stupid and immature enough to jump into bed with the first man you regard as *gorgeous*, we were obviously wrong.'

Flushing, Milly hit back. 'Oh, you've always been so prim and proper. If you're not careful you'll end up an old maid, or married to someone as narrow-minded as Trevor.'

'Suppose you leave me out of it.' Joanne tried to speak calmly. 'It's *your* future we're discussing…and Duncan's. He absolutely adores you. Have you thought what this will do to him?'

'I never wanted to hurt him,' Milly said unhappily. 'But I don't seem able to help myself. I keep thinking about this wonderful trip to Norway and what I'll lose if I don't go.'

'Try thinking about what you'll lose if you *do* go. A future with a good man who loves you, who'll stand by you; a home of your own, and a chance to make a life together in a beautiful part of the world…

'Suppose you give up all those things and this *wonderful trip* doesn't materialise?'

Seeing the uncertainty on her sister's young face, Joanne pressed home her advantage. 'You can't expect Duncan to wait around tamely to see whether his wife is going to Scotland with him, or to Scandinavia with another man.'

Milly bit her lip. 'I'll know by tonight if the trip's on. Brad's been away on business for over a week, but he said he'd be back this evening and if the Norway trip needed to go ahead he'd call me.'

'*Here?*'

'Yes. You see, there's not much time. If it is all systems go, we'll be travelling tomorrow morning.'

'What if he doesn't call?'

Milly twisted her wedding ring round and round her finger. 'I don't know. I may go to Scotland… I'm not sure—'

The sound of a key turning in the lock cut through her words, and a moment later a voice called cheerily, 'Milly, darling, I'm back.'

Scrambling to her feet, Milly said urgently, 'Jo, you won't say anything to Duncan until I've made up my mind?'

'Not a word. But if you don't want him to start asking awkward questions, I suggest that while I finish getting dinner ready you go up and make a start on some packing.'

As the girl hurried away, her bright-blue eyes clouded with worry, Joanne rose heavily to her feet and collected the cups and saucers.

Damn Brad Lancing! she thought violently as she rinsed and dried them. How *could* he encourage someone who was obviously just an easily-led young girl, and *married* into the bargain?

Milly might have imagined herself in love with him, but if he hadn't taken her out to dinner and dangled the bait of this Norwegian trip in front of her she wouldn't be seriously contemplating leaving Duncan.

Standing wringing the tea towel between her hands as though it was Brad Lancing's neck, Joanne was still mentally castigating him when the wall-phone, just by her head, rang.

She picked it up on the first ring and gave the number distractedly.

'Miss Winslow?' a clear, well-modulated voice asked.

'Yes.'

'Brad Lancing. The Norwegian trip is on. I'll be pleased if you'll have dinner with me tonight, so we can discuss the travel arrangements...?'

A red mist forming in front of her eyes and the blood pounding in her ears, Joanne was about to tell him who she was, and exactly what she thought of him, when a sudden sense of caution brought her up short.

Would that be wise?

Rather than giving up, a man like him, with no sense of shame, might only keep on trying to contact the girl he had obviously marked down as his next conquest, and somehow she must prevent that at all costs...

While her thoughts raced frantically, part of her mind registered the fact that the attractive voice was going on, 'I'll be at Somersby's at seven-thirty, if you can make it?'

About to say coldly that she couldn't, Joanne hesitated. Then, reasoning that if she agreed, as he doubtless expected, he would have no cause to argue or phone again, she adopted Milly's slightly breathy way of speaking, and said, 'Yes, I'll be there.'

'The address is Grant Street, Mayfair. Take a taxi.'

A second later she heard the receiver at the other end being replaced. It seemed he was a man of few words. Which was a blessing. If he'd tried to engage her in conversation it would have been difficult to keep up the pretence.

Even worse, Milly might have put in an appearance, and so long as she believed he hadn't rung she could well decide to go to Scotland.

Once there, and settled into her new life, surely this temporary infatuation would die a natural death?

Feeling somewhat more cheerful, Joanne went back to preparing the meal.

Everything was in the stove, and she had just started to set the table when a most unwelcome thought presented itself. Brad Lancing had said *Somersby's at seven-thirty*... If no one turned up, would he ring again to find out why?

Her blood ran cold. That could prove disastrous.

At seven-thirty they would still be sitting down to their meal, and, expecting him to ring, Milly would hardly hold back and let her sister fob him off.

Well, there was only one thing for it, Joanne decided; she would have to keep the appointment. At least it would give her a chance to tell him to his face just what she thought of men like him...

She heard the sound of the front door closing, and footsteps crossing the hall. A moment later Steve and his fiancée appeared in the doorway.

An inch or so under six feet, and slimly built, Steve was dark-haired and blue-eyed. With a thin, intelligent face and good features, he just missed out on being handsome.

But he was so genuinely *nice* that Joanne had often wondered why he hadn't been snapped up. Except he worked so hard that, until a few months ago, there had been no time for a woman in his life.

Then Lisa, small and blonde and as sweet as she was pretty, had come to work for him.

It had been love at first sight, and now with a baby on the way—unplanned, they had admitted sheepishly, but very much wanted—they were busy making arrangements for a late-October wedding.

Sniffing appreciatively, Steve said, 'Something smells

good.' Then with undisguised eagerness, 'How did things go with Liam Peters?'

'Monday morning, first thing, you can send in the troops.'

He gave a whoop of joy and, seizing hold of her, whirled her round until she was breathless.

'Looks as if you've had some good news,' Duncan remarked as he and Milly joined them.

'You're not wrong… And we're going to have a real celebration! There should be a couple of bottles of bubbly somewhere.'

'It's already in the fridge,' Joanne said.

'Clever girl!' Taking a bottle, Steve eased out the cork, poured the wine and, having handed a glass to each of the others, raised his own in salute.

'Here's to us, and particularly Jo, who's managed to swing the deal with Liam Peters, as well as finding time to take care of us all and cook some marvellous meals.'

There was a little burst of cheering, and they all drank. The bubbles made Milly sneeze, and then laugh.

Drawing a deep breath, Joanne took the plunge. 'I *hope* it's a marvellous meal tonight. I'm sorry to say I won't be here to share it.'

Seeing the surprise on all their faces, she added hurriedly, 'Trevor forgot it was tonight Milly and Duncan were leaving for Scotland, and he booked expensive seats at a special concert he knew I particularly wanted to go to.'

Perhaps the explanation was a little fulsome, but it was the truth, as far as it went.

What she failed to add was that, on discovering what he'd done, she had paid for her ticket—Trevor wasn't one to waste money—and suggested that he take his mother instead.

Milly, clearly disappointed, moved closer to her fair-haired husband, who put his arm around her.

Please God, things would work out, Joanne thought,

watching them together. Milly was too young to mess up her life.

'Well, if you won't be here on our last night,' Duncan said cheerfully, 'we shall expect you to be our first visitor when we get settled in.'

'Done!'

'Lisa's staying over,' Steve said; as he opened the second bottle of wine, 'so I won't need to turn out to drive her home…'

Afraid of being late in case Brad Lancing was the impatient sort who might call to see where she'd got to, Joanne left the others talking, and, having rung for a taxi, slipped upstairs to shower and change.

Needing to keep up the pretence of her concert-going, she put on her best silk suit, made up with care, fastened pearl studs onto her neat lobes, and swept her dark hair into an elegant chignon.

When she came down again, Duncan whistled, and Milly nodded approvingly. 'Not bad. Though I have to say it's wasted on Trevor.'

Then a little tremulously, 'Well, I guess we'll be gone before you get back…'

So she had decided to go. Joanne said a silent prayer of thanks.

With her emotions running high, and feeling the prick of tears behind her eyes, she hugged her sister and brother-in-law and said as brightly as possible, 'Have a good journey… And as soon as you're ready for visitors, let me know.'

'Will do,' Duncan assured her.

The doorbell announced the arrival of the taxi, and after more quick hugs all round, Joanne said, 'Well, enjoy your meal,' and fled before she could disgrace herself by crying.

Somersby's proved to be a select and stylish restaurant above an art gallery. The taxi dropped Joanne at the awninged entrance, and, her heart beating fast, she climbed a flight of red-carpeted stairs.

At the top, a uniformed attendant was waiting to open the heavy glass doors for her.

As she crossed the luxurious foyer she went over in her mind all the things she intended to say to Brad Lancing. When she had, hopefully, made him squirm, she would walk out.

No, that wasn't the way to do it. It would be almost three hours before Milly and Duncan started for the station, and in that time, left to his own devices, Lancing might phone and throw a spanner in the works.

She just couldn't chance it. Somehow she needed to keep him occupied until Milly was safely on the train.

But how?

That still undecided, Joanne found herself facing another dilemma. She had no idea what he looked like. She pictured him as floridly handsome, with bold eyes and a sensual mouth. Possibly even a moustache.

Apart from Duncan, who was good-looking in a boyish, wholesome way, she and Milly had never shared the same taste in men, Milly tending to go for the more blatantly sexual.

Oh, well, if she just walked in, hopefully there wouldn't be too many men sitting alone waiting for their dates. But it was only seven-twenty-five; suppose he hadn't yet arrived?

As she hesitated in the doorway, the *maître d'* appeared at her elbow. 'Good evening, madam.'

'Good evening. I'm joining a Mr Lancing.'

Inclining his head, he murmured, 'If you'll come this way?'

Rehearsing in her mind what she was going to say, Joanne followed as he led the way to a small, secluded table in an alcove, where a man with thick dark hair was sitting.

He glanced up at their approach, and then rose politely to his feet.

Over six feet tall and broad-shouldered, his face lean and tanned and, apart from a certain toughness, almost ascetic, he was so unlike the florid, thickset man she had visualised that for a moment she wondered confusedly if the waiter had made a mistake.

But, stopping by the table, he murmured discreetly, 'Your guest, Mr Lancing.'

Somehow Brad Lancing's appearance threw her, and instead of the words she had been rehearsing, wits completely scattered, she found herself stammering, 'M-Mr Lancing... I'm Miss Winslow...but, as you see, the wrong one.'

He raised dark, well-marked brows. 'Not the one I was expecting, admittedly, but equally charming.'

Hating him on sight, she explained a shade breathlessly, 'I'm Milly's sister.'

'You're nothing at all like her,' he observed dispassionately.

'No.'

'Won't you sit down?'

'Thank you.'

He remained on his feet until the *maître d'* had pulled out her chair and settled her, before resuming his own seat.

At least the brute had manners, she conceded.

'I'm afraid I'm the bringer of bad tidings,' she said as soon as they were alone.

His eyes were every bit as fascinating as Milly had said. A clear dark green, and put in with a sooty finger, they made her breath quicken as they rested on her face. 'Nothing too dreadful, I hope?'

'Milly can't come,' she informed him in a rush.

'I see.' Then like a rattlesnake striking, 'You're the Miss Winslow I spoke to on the phone.'

Shaken by his perspicacity, she found herself admitting, 'W-well, yes.'

'In that case you're not the wrong one at all.' He smiled a little, drawing her attention to his mouth.

Firm and controlled, yet passionate, it had a combination of warm sensuality and cool austereness that might have made almost any woman drool, and Joanne realised all too clearly why Milly fancied herself in love with him.

She was dragging her gaze away with an effort, when he said softly, 'Tell me, Miss Winslow, why did you pretend to be your sister?'

'I—I didn't…'

Ignoring her instinctive denial, he insisted, 'Of course you did. You even imitated her voice.'

Weakly, Joanne said, 'It was just a joke… She wasn't there, and I…'

'You were simply answering for her?'

'Yes.'

'Do you always answer for your sister?'

'No, of course not… But I knew she'd want to come…'

'So why isn't she here?'

'Well, just before she was due to start, she had an emergency call from an elderly aunt,' Joanne improvised wildly. 'Poor Aunt Alice had just had a bad fall and was refusing to go into hospital. Milly is very fond of her…'

Just for an instant Joanne thought she saw a gleam of unholy amusement in those clear green eyes, but his face showed no trace of a smile as he said, 'I know how these family relationships can be.'

'She wasn't sure how long it would take to get Auntie settled,' Joanne ploughed on, 'and she thought she might possibly have to stay the night.'

'So you came in her place?'

'Well, yes… I thought I'd better come and explain in person.'

'Much nicer and more *friendly* than simply phoning,' he agreed drily.

It was quite obvious what he was thinking, and suddenly she knew exactly how to play it.

Desperate situations called for desperate measures. If she could flatter his ego, pander to his vanity, make him believe she fancied him, he might ask her to have dinner with him.

If he did she should be able to string him along until Milly was safely out of his clutches. *Then* she would have the pleasure of telling him exactly what she thought of him.

Trying for a spot of girlish confusion, she admitted, 'I must confess, I've been hoping to meet you.'

'Really?' he murmured, a glint in his eye.

'I've heard such a lot about you from Milly.'

A look she couldn't decipher crossed his face, before he asked ironically, 'Can any secretary be relied on to say good things about her boss?'

'Surely that depends on the boss?' Joanne's answer was a little sharp, and, reminding herself of the role she had decided to play, she gave him a coy glance from beneath long, silky lashes, and added, 'If he happens to be a man like you…'

As though genuinely curious, he asked, 'So what exactly did…Milly…say about me?'

'She said you were clever, charismatic, and totally charming.'

Just for an instant he looked disconcerted. Then he observed lightly, 'I might find that description difficult to live up to. However,' he went on with a touch of self-mockery, 'rather than let the ''world of bosses'' down, I'll try…'

At that moment one of the waiters came up and handed them both a leather-covered menu.

'Oh…' Joanne made to rise. 'I really ought to go and let you have your meal in peace.'

He asked, as she'd been hoping he would, 'Won't you stay and dine with me?'

'Well, I...'

'Unless your fiancé would object?'

He had sharp eyes, she thought as she answered, 'No, I'm sure he wouldn't.'

'Then please, do stay.'

'Thank you, I'd like to.' She made no attempt to hide the eagerness.

'Would you care for a drink while you look at the menu? Champagne, perhaps?'

The glass of wine she had drunk earlier, combined with all the emotional turmoil, had made her feel strangely light-headed, but she managed a smile, and agreed, 'That would be lovely.'

He signalled the wine waiter and gave the order.

Within moments, the man was back with a bottle of the finest champagne in an ice bucket. Having gently twirled the bottle for a moment or two, he removed the wiring, eased out the cork, and poured the smoking wine into two flutes, before departing soft-footed.

Joanne was watching the bubbles rise, when her companion raised his glass and, his eyes smiling into hers, said softly, 'Here's to an exciting evening.'

She smiled back, and took a cautious sip. With a bit of luck he would get more excitement than he'd bargained for!

CHAPTER TWO

PLAYING for time, Joanne sipped her champagne and scanned the menu for as long as she dared, before choosing a melon starter and a main course of avocado and prawns.

The order given, Brad Lancing fixed her with his handsome eyes, and asked, 'By the way, as your sister's spokeswoman, can you tell me if she still intends to go on this Norwegian trip?'

Caught wrong-footed, Joanne hesitated, then said lamely, 'Well, I think she'd like to.'

Picking up on that uncertainty, he explained, 'You see, there's not much time. I have two seats booked on a plane that leaves Heathrow at lunch time, and if your sister is likely to be still tied up with…your auntie I shall need to find myself another secretary.'

And one who was willing to be his bed-companion, no doubt, Joanne thought sourly.

Hoping to give him as much trouble as possible, she assured him, 'I'm quite sure Milly won't want to let you down.'

Recklessly, she added, 'And if by any chance she can't come, I might even volunteer for the post myself!'

A devilish gleam in his eye, he refilled her glass and said, 'I might hold you to that. But you'd need to come prepared. The nights can get pretty chilly.'

'Oh, I'm sure I could cope.'

'Have you much experience?'

Loathing both him and the *double entendre*, she gave him a come-hither look and cooed, 'Oh, yes, lots.'

'Where are you working now?'

Reluctant to provide too much personal information, she said briefly, 'Optima Business Services.'

'Owned by Steven Winslow.'

It was a statement not a question, but she answered, 'That's right.'

Brad Lancing seemed to know a great deal. But perhaps Milly had told him?

'So you act as your brother's secretary?' he pursued evenly.

'I've been Steve's personal assistant for over five years.'

Reacting to her tone, he said, 'I see.' Then, a challenge in his voice, 'And are you a good PA?'

'If I wasn't I wouldn't have kept the job. Neither of us believes in nepotism.'

As soon as the words were out it struck her that she had been replying as *herself*, rather than the kind of woman she was pretending to be.

Giving him a flirtatious glance, she said in her best girly voice, 'But *I'm* not very interesting… I'd much rather talk about *you*, Mr Lancing.'

His firm mouth twitched. 'Won't you call me Brad?'

'I'd love to, if you call me Joanne.'

'It will be my pleasure.'

Taking a sip of her champagne, she smiled at him over the rim of the glass. Then, recalling something Milly had once said, she leaned towards him and murmured in a husky voice, 'I've always found handsome, powerful men like you a real turn-on.'

The 'like you' was her own contribution.

An expression that might have been amusement flitted across his face, making her wonder if she was overdoing it, but it was gone in an instant, and she decided it must have been self-satisfaction.

Someone as vain and egotistical as he undoubtedly was would lap up any amount of flattery.

He must have been looking forward to a romantic evening with a girl who thought he was wonderful, and being a womaniser, he would no doubt have seduction on his mind.

Well, let him believe she was a pushover. The shock would be all the greater when he discovered that instead of the sex kitten he was hoping for, she was a cat with claws.

For the next hour or so, while they ate what turned out to be a very good meal, Joanne flirted with him shamelessly. Hanging on his every word, she touched his sleeve from time to time and occasionally let her foot nudge his under the table.

Avoiding questions about herself as much as possible, she made an effort to keep the conversation centred on him.

It proved to be harder than she had anticipated.

Most men, even the nicest ones, were usually happy to keep their egos inflated by talking about themselves, but Brad Lancing, while prepared to discuss the business scene, seemed unwilling to divulge anything remotely personal.

Perhaps he was married after all?

If he was, she pitied his poor wife.

'I suppose you must travel an awful lot?' Joanne enquired as the waiter brought the liqueur coffees Brad had ordered.

'Not as much as I used to. These days I only travel if I believe my presence is really essential.'

'Your wife must be pleased about that,' she remarked idly, taking a sip of her coffee.

Those green eyes pinned her, making her go oddly fluttery. 'I'm not married,' he told her coolly, 'nor have I ever been remotely tempted to put my head in the silken noose.'

'Oh…'

With a gleam of mockery, he added, 'Who was it said, "Love all and marry none"?'

'Whoever it was, I understand you follow their advice to the letter?' The sharp words were out before she could prevent them.

'I have until now,' he admitted easily. Then with a side-long glance, 'You sound as if you disapprove?'

She answered the question with another. 'Who was it said, "Gather ye rosebuds while ye may"?'

'Now, that one I *can* answer. Herrick.'

His voice, as well as being attractive, was educated, but, not having put him down as a man who would take much interest in poetry, she was surprised by his knowledge.

'Do you agree with the sentiment?' he pursued.

'I suppose so,' she admitted, 'though I haven't had much time for gathering rosebuds.'

'Why not?'

She replied briefly, 'When our parents died in a train crash I left college to take over the running of the house.'

'How old were you then?'

'Nineteen.'

'And you went to work for your brother at the same time?'

'Yes.'

'How many were there in the family?'

'Just three. Steve, who's the eldest, myself, and Milly, who was only a schoolgirl.'

'So you've been a mother to your younger sister?'

'You could say that.'

Seeing he was about to probe further, she forced a bright smile, and changed the subject. 'I understand that you'll be in Norway for six weeks or so?'

'That's right.'

'It seems a long time for a business trip. Are you planning a new project?'

'No. Just sorting out a family business that's been in existence for generations.'

'A family business?' she echoed in surprise. 'Surely Lancing isn't a Norwegian name?'

'No, it was my mother who came from Norway. Her father was Norwegian and her mother English. An only child, she lived with her parents in Bergen until she met and married my father.

'After that she only returned to Norway for holidays, though the family remained close until she was killed in an accident just over a year ago.

'When my grandfather died shortly afterwards he left me the Dragon Shipping Line and hotel business he'd spent his entire life running.

'Since then there have been quite a few problems, and a while ago I sent one of my best men over there to deal with them.

'Paul was fairly sure he was well on his way to sorting them out without needing me, but during the last couple of months things have started to go wrong again.

'Then this morning something more serious happened that made up his mind that he needed my help, and he contacted me to say he thinks I should go after all.

'If the problems *had* been resolved I would probably have left my trip until the spring. But as it is, I can't let things drift until then.'

Starting to feel more than a little woozy, she asked, 'Why spring?'

'Because, though September is a wonderful time to hike in the hills, Norway is particularly beautiful in the spring when the ice is breaking up and the rivers are in spate...

'You see, as well as dealing with the business side, it's my intention to take some time off and have a break.

'Due to pressure of work I haven't had a proper holiday for a couple of years, and I haven't been to Norway for more than a few days at a time on business.

'I'm very fond of my mother's homeland, so the thought of taking a real holiday there is an enticing prospect...'

Enticing enough to almost make Milly leave her husband, Joanne thought bitterly.

He raised a winged brow. 'Judging by your expression, you don't think so?'

'Not at all,' she disagreed hastily. 'I've always thought Norway must be wonderful. Which part are you going to?'

'Bergen. Have you ever been there?'

'No.'

'Have you done much travelling?'

'Not since my parents died. Though I did have a long-weekend break earlier this year.'

'Where did you choose to go?'

'I was hoping to go to Rome, but Trevor favoured Amsterdam.' Now, what on earth had made her tell him that?

Picking up her left hand, he examined the diamond solitaire she wore. 'Trevor being your fiancé?'

After a brief hesitation, she said, 'Yes.'

He stroked over her knuckles with his thumb, sending a shiver through her. 'But obviously he's not the jealous type?'

'No.' Restive beneath his touch, she withdrew her hand, and glanced a shade muzzily at her watch. Milly and Duncan should be away from the house in the next five minutes or so…

'You seem eager to leave,' Brad commented lightly.

She was. Her mission accomplished, she couldn't wait to end the charade and escape. 'Well, if you need to make a fairly early start tomorrow…'

'Yes, you're quite right,' he agreed, signalling the waiter. 'It's time we were making a move.'

High time. Drawing a deep breath, she turned to tell him exactly what she thought of him, but just at that instant the waiter arrived.

While Brad paid the bill, and added a generous tip, she glanced around. There were still quite a few people within earshot, and, disliking the idea of making a scene in the quiet restaurant, she decided to wait until they were outside.

When she had picked up her bag he drew back her chair, and she rose to her feet a shade unsteadily. A hand cupping her elbow, he escorted her out of the restaurant and across the foyer.

Distinctly light-headed, she had to make herself concentrate as they descended the red-carpeted stairs. A couple of steps from the bottom, she stumbled, and he was forced to steady her.

At the entrance, a sleek grey limousine was drawn up, a liveried chauffeur holding open the door. Before Joanne could gather her wits Brad had handed her in and was sitting beside her.

'I'd intended to get a taxi,' she said in belated and breathless protest as they drew away.

'Oh?'

Without turning his head, the chauffeur asked, 'Straight home, sir?'

'Yes, please, Gregory.' Brad touched a button and the glass partition between the driver and his passengers closed. A moment later blinds slid into place, covering both the partition and the windows.

Taking immediate advantage of the softly lit intimacy, he caressed her silk-clad knee.

Flinching away in a sudden panic, and wishing desperately that she hadn't been foolish enough to get into the car in the first place, Joanne announced as firmly as possible, 'I live in Fulham, and I—'

'Yes, I know.' He drew her close, and an instant later his mouth was covering hers.

Shocked by the suddenness of the move and by the tumult of feeling his kiss evoked, for a moment or two she made no attempt to free herself.

When, remembering just *who* was kissing her, she pulled herself together and began to struggle, his arms merely tightened and he deepened the kiss.

Terrified now, she began to struggle in earnest, but he was so much stronger than she had realised, and he held her easily.

Tearing her mouth free, she gasped, 'Leave me alone. I don't want you to touch me…'

Looking completely unruffled, he remarked, 'From the way you've been behaving, I rather thought you were inviting it.'

'Well, you were wrong. I want to go home,' she added shakily.

'That's where we are going.'

'*My* home,' she insisted.

'Somehow I'd got the impression that, in spite of being engaged, you'd intended to come home with me.'

Her heart throwing itself against her ribs, she said hoarsely, 'Well, you were wrong! I'd like you to tell your chauffeur to stop and let me get out right this minute.'

Raising his dark brows in mock-surprise, he queried, 'So what made you change your mind?'

'I haven't *changed my mind*. I—'

'I'm pleased to hear it.'

Ignoring the interruption, she rushed on, 'I haven't *changed my mind* because I never had the slightest intention of going home with you.'

His voice holding more than a hint of soft menace, he said, 'I wouldn't like to think you'd been leading me on just for the hell of it.'

She swallowed hard. 'I haven't been leading you on just for the hell of it—'

'Well, as you have undoubtedly been leading me on, perhaps you'd like to tell me why?'

'Because I needed to keep you occupied, to prevent you contacting Milly,' she admitted in a rush.

He smiled grimly. 'So your sister was at home all the time? Oddly enough I never did believe in poor Auntie Alice…

'But I'm afraid I don't understand why you were prepared to go to such lengths to stop me contacting my own secretary?'

'If you *had* spoken to her she would have dropped everything and come.'

'I see,' he said slowly. 'And you thought she might be…keeping my bed warm tonight?'

'I know she would.'

'You don't know anything of the kind.'

'She's infatuated with you.'

'And you blame me for that?'

'Of course I blame you. She told me how you'd taken her out to dinner, and the way you'd looked at her.

'If I hadn't discovered what was going on, and happened to intercept your phone call, she would have risked everything to be here.'

He frowned. 'Risked everything?'

Into her stride now, Joanne rushed on, 'Steve told me you had a rotten reputation as far as women were concerned, but I never dreamt that even a swine like you would go after a girl who's only eighteen and married into the bargain—'

'Married?' He sounded startled.

'Don't pretend you didn't know.'

Her face full of contempt, she lashed out at him verbally. 'You're a miserable, womanising bastard, and totally without principles!

'You dangled the bait of a Norwegian trip in front of her until she was almost prepared to break up her marriage and go to Norway with you, rather than move to Scotland with her husband—'

'Would you care to slow down a little…? I'm getting confused. I thought she lived with you?'

'She does, and so does her husband… Or rather they *did*. They'll soon be on their way to Edinburgh to live, and hopefully Milly will be well out of reach of lecherous men like you…' Running out of breath, Joanne stopped abruptly.

'Now I'm beginning to understand,' Brad said evenly.

'Presumably they're taking the night sleeper, and you wanted to keep me occupied until your sister was safely on board and couldn't change her mind…'

'That's right.' Joanne made no secret of her triumph. 'Now, if you'll ask your chauffeur to stop and let me get out…'

When he made no move she threatened shakily, 'If you don't I'll start screaming.'

Calmly, he said, 'Even if I allowed you to scream, I doubt very much if anyone would hear…'

Recalling both his strength and his total lack of scruples, she shuddered.

'And I can't help but feel you owe me…'

When she said nothing he pointed out, 'You seem quite certain that your sister would have been sharing my bed tonight.'

'Well, I'm not Milly,' she cried desperately.

'But earlier you agreed that you'd come in her place. You even boasted that you were experienced.'

Watching all the colour drain from her face, he observed mockingly, 'Now you're acting more like a frightened schoolgirl than a woman with lots of experience.'

He ran his hand up her thigh and, his voice smooth as satin, queried, 'You did say ''lots''?'

She pushed his hand away, and seeing the gleam in his eye, realised he was enjoying baiting her, getting a little of his own back.

Suddenly afraid of how far he'd go, she begged, 'Please don't.'

'That's better,' he applauded.

'Will you let me get out?' Despite all her efforts her voice shook betrayingly as she added, '*Please.*'

His dark, well-shaped head tilted a little to one side, he pretended to consider. Then he said ironically, 'As you're asking so prettily, and I don't want to add kidnapping to my list of crimes, I'll be happy to take you home. Where do you live, exactly?'

She gave him her address.

He pressed a button, and, speaking into a small grille, ordered, 'Gregory, I'd like you to go straight to Fulham and drop Miss Winslow at twenty three Carlisle Street.'

'Thank you,' she said through gritted teeth.

Settling himself back into his seat, Brad turned to her and asked seriously, 'Suppose I told you that you're totally mistaken about my relationship with your sister? That as far as I'm concerned she's simply a nice girl and an efficient secretary?'

So now he was trying to excuse himself, make himself out to be whiter than white.

As she remembered the way he had slid his hand up her thigh Joanne's blood boiled.

'Knowing what kind of man you are, I wouldn't believe a word of it,' she said contemptuously, and moved as far away from him as the seat would allow.

For a while they sat in a silence that, keyed-up as she was, soon became nerve-racking. Bracing herself, she stole a sideways look at his clear-cut profile.

It was cold and set, and she realised that he was quietly, but furiously, angry.

But then he was not only a man whose lies had been summarily rejected, but also a hunter deprived of his prey.

Serve him right, she thought with immense satisfaction. Let him go to bed frustrated for once.

He turned his head and glanced at her. As he caught sight of her gleeful expression, his own face hardened even more.

At that precise moment the limousine slowed down, drew into the kerb, and stopped.

The instant the chauffeur opened the door, Joanne scrambled out without a backward glance, only to find Brad close on her heels as she crossed the broad pavement.

Accompanying her up the steps, he waited impassively

in the lamp-lit porch while she found her key, then, taking it from her nerveless fingers, he opened the door.

'Thank you.' Her voice was cold, and, dropping the key back into her bag, she turned away.

'Before you go,' Brad said silkily, 'in view of the expectations you raised, I think at the very least I'm entitled to a goodnight kiss.'

Stepping over the threshold, he pinned her back against the door panels.

'Get your hands off me, you—'

Ignoring her protest, he covered her mouth with his and kissed her deeply.

His kiss was insolent, punitive, and by the time he finally lifted his head she was dazed and breathless.

Looking down into eyes that brimmed with tears of rage, he said, 'As you're convinced I'm a lecherous, unfeeling brute, I thought you'd be disappointed if I didn't act like one.'

As he moved back she lifted her hand and slapped his face as hard as she could. Then, catching her breath in a kind of sob, she fled into the house, banging the door behind her.

Trembling in every limb, she sank down limply onto the hall chair, and, taking a tissue from her bag, scrubbed repeatedly at her lips, as if trying to remove every last trace of his kiss.

Damn Brad Lancing to hell! she thought furiously as she listened to the car door slam and the limousine drive away. He had to be the most obnoxious man she had ever met, and if she never saw him again it would be too soon. He was immoral and arrogant and quite unscrupulous...

Seething futilely, she sat mentally flaying him, until the worst of her agitation had subsided and she had returned to a state of relative calm.

Everywhere was quiet and, apart from the hallway, the house seemed to be in darkness. Presuming that Steve and

Lisa had gone to bed, she bolted the door and made her way upstairs.

As she reached the landing Steve's bedroom door opened. 'I know this sounds dead nosy,' he admitted with an unrepentant grin, 'but we happened to see you getting out of a posh limousine…'

Oh, hell! Joanne thought helplessly. In the circumstances, the last thing she wanted was to have to explain where she had been, and why.

It wouldn't be fair to tell anyone else about Milly's involvement, especially now everything was, hopefully, going to be all right.

'I can't imagine it belonged to Trevor?' Steve pursued.

'No,' she said after a moment.

As Lisa appeared at his elbow he added, 'The man who got out with you…while not in the least like Trevor, looked strangely familiar…'

'Did he?' she stonewalled.

'Though I've only seen him once—Milly pointed him out one day when I picked her up from work—he's not a man one would easily forget…'

When she said nothing, his voice teasing, Steve urged, 'Come on, Sis, give. Can't you see we're both dying of curiosity to know what you were doing out with Brad Lancing?'

Caught off balance, and unable to think of any satisfactory explanation, she admitted boldly, 'I was having dinner with him.'

Steve whistled softly. 'So you were *lying* about Trevor and the concert tickets?'

'Not exactly. He did get some tickets, but I told him I couldn't go.'

Frowning, Steve said, 'I know the engagement isn't *official* but this isn't like you, Sis…'

Joanne groaned inwardly. Now, on top of everything else, Steve thought she was cheating on Trevor.

She wished, not for the first time, that, even at the risk of hurting his feelings, she had refused point-blank to wear Trevor's ring until she had come to a firm decision.

When she said nothing, sounding baffled, Steve commented, 'I didn't even realise you knew Lancing.'

'I only met him recently.'

'Why did you...? No, don't tell me, I can guess why you kept it a secret. You didn't want to upset Milly when she'd developed this schoolgirl crush on the guy...'

So Steve had been aware of Milly's infatuation, but, judging by his casual tone, he hadn't appreciated what terrible consequences there might have been.

But, showing he *had*, he went on, 'The trouble is, men like him aren't to be trusted. If he'd turned on the heat things could have been difficult, to say the least.'

Then awkwardly, 'I know it's none of my business, Sis, but if you intend to go on seeing Lancing you will take care, won't you?'

'I'm almost twenty-five,' she pointed out a shade tartly. 'Old enough to know what I'm doing...'

That was a laugh.

'And if it sets your mind at rest, I'm unlikely to be seeing him again. Tomorrow he's going to Norway for six weeks on business.'

Briskly, she added, 'Now I'm off to bed. Goodnight, you two.'

Escaping into her own room, she closed the door firmly behind her, and went through to the bathroom to strip off her clothes.

What a night! she thought wearily. The only thing she could hope was that she had managed to discomfit Brad Lancing as much as he had annoyed her.

Rather than falling for him, as Steve seemed to fear, she had found him hateful and despicable. The few hours spent in his company were some of the worst she had ever had to endure.

Remembering the unpleasant little scene in the car, the way he had run his hand up her thigh and, his voice smooth as satin, queried, 'You did say "lots"?' she shuddered. He had deliberately gone out of his way to frighten and humiliate her.

Joanne brushed out her long dark hair and pulled on a voluminous cotton nightie, before cleaning her teeth more vigorously than usual.

Then, climbing into bed, she switched off the light, closed her eyes, and endeavoured to put Brad Lancing right out of her mind.

After more than an hour she was still wide awake and, in spite of all her efforts, still thinking about him, repeatedly going over in her mind everything he had said and done.

Especially that last devastating kiss.

She could still recall the way his mouth had ruthlessly mastered hers; smell the subtle scent of his aftershave; taste the hint of liqueur and the freshness of his breath; feel the way every nerve in her body had tightened in response.

Just thinking about it was enough to stir her senses and, she was horrified to realise, make a core of liquid heat start to form in the pit of her stomach.

No! She tried hard to deny it. How could a man like that, a man she both loathed and despised, arouse a desire that a decent, upright man like Trevor had never been able to awaken?

It was *unthinkable*.

Disturbed and wholly dismayed, she tossed and turned restlessly, finally drifting into an uneasy doze around dawn.

Joanne was trawled from the depths by a persistent sound that it took her a moment or two to identify as the doorbell.

It was almost certainly the postman, who was tending to come early these days, and she didn't want Steve to be disturbed. Working as hard as he did, he liked to sleep late at the weekend.

Stumbling groggily out of bed, she pulled on her dressing gown and, tying the belt around her slender waist, padded barefoot down the stairs.

All the time the bell kept ringing with a maddening persistence that grated on her nerves. So much *noise*, and he probably only wanted to deliver one of those aggravating packets that gave themselves importance by saying, 'Please do not bend…' and then contained just junk mail.

Having drawn back the bolts, she threw open the door, and burst out crossly, 'Will you please stop ringing the bell? My brother's still in bed and…'

The words died on her lips.

Brad Lancing was standing there wearing a well-cut suit and a matching shirt and tie. Freshly shaved, his thick, dark hair parted on the left and neatly brushed, his green eyes clear and sparkling with health, he looked dangerously attractive and virile.

Before she could slam the door in his face he took his finger off the bell-push, and strolled in as if he owned the place.

As, the wind taken completely out of her sails, Joanne stepped back, he closed the door behind him and stood gazing down at her, his six-foot frame easily dwarfing her.

Straight-faced, he studied her shiny nose, the dark, silky hair tumbling round her shoulders, her demure Victorian nightdress and gown, her slim bare feet, and commented, 'Just up, I see.'

Infuriated by his obvious amusement, she demanded, 'What are you doing here?'

'Can't you guess?'

'It's too early in the morning for guessing games,' she informed him curtly, 'so perhaps you wouldn't mind just telling me what you want?'

His eyes glinted at her tone. 'You.'

'What?' she said stupidly.

'I'll be setting off for Norway around lunch time today, and I need a secretary. As it's the weekend and too late to make other arrangements, I've decided to accept your offer.'

'Offer? What offer?'

'Surely you remember offering, "If by any chance Milly can't come, I might volunteer for the post myself"?'

'I wasn't serious.' She took a step backwards and, a panicky edge to her voice, repeated, 'Of course I wasn't serious.'

His dark, winged brows drew together in a frown. 'That's a pity, because when I said I might hold you to it, I *was*.

'Now, clearly your sister isn't in any position to come, so the job's yours.'

Knowing he'd noted that touch of panic, and determined to stay cool, Joanne said, 'Thanks, but I already have a job.'

'I'm sure that, for the next six weeks or so, your brother could find himself another PA.'

With polite finality, she said, 'Even if he could, I wouldn't be taking up your offer.'

The door to the kitchen was ajar, and, glancing in at the comfortable-looking high-backed chairs drawn up in front of the stove, Brad suggested, 'Rather than stand here, suppose we go through and have some coffee while we talk about it?'

'I've no intention of making you coffee, and I don't want to talk about it.'

Stepping past him, she held open the front door. 'Now, if you'll please leave.'

When he made no move to go, losing her cool, she cried, 'Go on, get out! If you don't leave this instant I'll call Steve and get him to throw you out.'

'Are you sure that's wise?'

Though his tone was mild, it was undoubtedly a threat,

and she hesitated. There was something about his firm
mouth, the set of his jaw that, despite his quiet manner, his
veneer of charm, made him formidable.

She shivered.

Steve was far from being a seven-stone weakling, but
she sensed instinctively that he would be no match for this
man.

As she stood irresolute, Brad Lancing took control once
more. Closing the door, he put a hand beneath her elbow
and urged her towards the kitchen.

Digging in her toes, she said mutinously, 'As far as I'm
concerned, there's nothing to talk about. You are the last
person in the world I would choose to work for.'

He shook his head almost regretfully. 'Ah, but you see,
you don't have a choice. At least not if you care what
happens to Steve's company.'

'What do you mean, "care what happens to Steve's company"? Of course I care.' She was aware that the note of
panic was back in her voice.

'Then we do have something to talk about.'

He strode into the kitchen, leaving her to follow in his
wake, demanding anxiously, 'What *could* happen to Steve's
company?'

Ignoring the question, he asked, 'Would you like to make
some coffee?'

'I've already told you, I wouldn't.'

He indicated one of the armchairs. 'Then perhaps you'd
like to sit down?'

'I don't want to sit down. I want to know what you're
talking about.'

Plugging in the electric kettle, he began to calmly assem-
ble the cafetière and mugs. 'When we're both sitting down
with a cup of coffee, I'll be happy to explain.'

CHAPTER THREE

SEEING he meant to have his way, she bit her lip and sat down, watching him with angry eyes.

His movements were deft, assured as he spooned coffee into the cafetière and filled it with water. She wondered abstractedly how such a masculine man could look so at home in a kitchen.

It was the last thing she had expected.

A lot of wealthy men with a staff of servants to wait on them had probably never even seen the inside of a kitchen.

As though aware of her hostile scrutiny, he turned and cocked an eyebrow at her. 'Milk and sugar?'

'Just milk, please.' She forced herself to answer civilly.

He handed her a mug of coffee and, putting his own on the stove where he could reach it, sat down in one of the high-backed chairs and regarded her quizzically.

Because he was well-groomed and smartly dressed, with her hair tumbling round her shoulders she felt dishevelled, and at a distinct disadvantage in what Milly referred to as her 'little orphan Annie' garb.

In a reflex action, she tucked her bare feet beneath her voluminous skirts, and saw him smile.

Gritting her teeth, she said as calmly as possible, 'Now you've got what you wanted and we're both sitting down with a cup of coffee, perhaps you'll tell me what could possibly happen to Steve?'

Brad answered with a question of his own. 'I understand your brother's having a hard struggle to keep his company afloat?'

'What makes you think that?'

'It's true isn't it?'

'It *was* true. But now things are looking up.'

'Really?' he drawled.

'Yes, really! Not only has Steve found an investment company willing to put money into Optima, but we've also just secured a contract to install a large new communications network.'

'For Liam Peters?'

Wondering how he knew, unless Milly had told him about the negotiations, she said, 'Yes.'

'What would your brother do if both those opportunities were to fall through?'

A chill running down her spine, she demanded, 'Why should they fall through?'

As though she hadn't spoken, Brad went on smoothly, 'With the house mortgaged up to the hilt, and scarcely enough money in hand to pay the staff their next month's wages—'

'Who told you that?' she broke in angrily.

'After I'd dropped you off last night I spent a little while checking up—'

'Well, wherever you got the information—'

'I got it from the horse's mouth, so to speak.'

'I don't know what you mean.'

'You've just told me your brother was promised a loan by an investment company?'

'Yes.' Shaken as she was by a sudden nameless fear, her voice was barely above a whisper.

'Before agreeing to lend a business money, the first thing an investment company does is obtain a very clear picture of their client's current financial situation, as well as the business's future prospects. MBL is no exception—'

'How do you know it was MBL…?' Almost before the words were out, she froze.

Watching the dawning look of horror in her deep blue eyes, he waited quietly.

With a courage he was forced to admire, she sat up straighter and lifted her chin. 'What does the M stand for?'

'Michael. Though the family have always used my middle name.'

'You don't happen to own Liam Peters too?'

'It's a subsidiary of Lancing International.'

'But surely you don't control their policies, or interfere in their internal decisions?'

'Not normally. But if I wanted to, all it would take is a word in the right ear.'

While the full enormity of what he was saying sank in she sat staring straight ahead, feeling curiously numb and empty.

She could hear herself asserting 'You are the last person in the world I would choose to work for'.

And his response: 'Ah, but, you see, you don't have a choice. At least not if you care what happens to Steve's company'.

After a moment she said carefully, 'There must be more ethical ways to acquire a secretary?'

'I'm sure there are. But, as I don't want just *any* secretary, it's a case of needs must…'

'You see, as this will be part-holiday, I want not only an efficient PA, but also a companion. I don't find there's much pleasure eating alone, sightseeing alone, spending the evenings alone…'

So this was what Milly had been asked for.

'I'd like someone intelligent to talk to, someone to share things with—'

'If you mean your bed, I won't sleep with you,' she broke in sharply. 'I won't be your mistress.'

He laid it on the line. 'If you really want to save your brother, you'll do anything I want you to do. Be anything I want you to be.'

'I've got a fiancé.'

'That didn't seem to worry you last night.'

Head bent, she clenched her hands together until the knuckles showed white. Then, looking up, her eyes so dark they appeared almost black, she moistened dry lips, and asked, 'Why me?'

He laughed, as though that was a silly question.

And perhaps, in the circumstances, it was.

'Shall we call it poetic justice? You deprived me of a perfectly good secretary—'

'But Milly wasn't free to—'

Taking no notice of the interruption, he went on relentlessly, 'And with no personal knowledge of what kind of man I really am, you attacked and reviled me.

'I'm afraid I don't take kindly to being called a lecher and a liar, and my motto has always been, "Don't get mad, get even."'

And this was his way of doing it. To use and humiliate her.

Feeling as though her blood had turned to ice in her veins, she shivered, seeing now, with hindsight, that it had been playing with dynamite to incense a man as ruthless as Brad Lancing.

Of course, he *might* be bluffing. For an instant she clung to the thought. But if she refused, and he *wasn't*, it would not only be the end of the company Steve had worked so hard to make successful, but the end of the road for them all.

There weren't that many jobs about. With no money coming in they would find it impossible to keep up the high mortgage payments…

Added to that, it might well put the young couple's wedding plans in jeopardy, and with a baby on the way the whole situation could become a nightmare…

And it would be all her fault.

If only she had had more sense…

But it was too late for regrets, and, having got into this

mess, how could she let Steve and Lisa and the loyal, hard-working staff at Optima suffer because of *her* stupidity?

The answer was, she couldn't.

If she hadn't meddled in the first place she would never have met Brad Lancing and none of this would have happened… But something even worse *might* have done.

At this very moment, Milly, rather than being safely in Scotland, might be wrecking not only her own life but also Duncan's, by going to Norway with a womanising swine who would drop her the minute he had had his fun.

It didn't bear thinking about. At least *this* way there would only be herself who would suffer…

She had looked up to give Brad Lancing her answer, when the door opened and Steve walked into the kitchen wearing a short navy-blue towelling robe.

Barefoot, his dark hair rumpled, he rubbed the back of his neck and yawned widely. 'I could do with a coffee if there's any made?'

'There should be some in the pot.' She was surprised by how steady her voice sounded.

'Thanks. Lisa's still asleep so I'll…' The words tailed off as he caught sight of Brad. 'Sorry, I didn't realise you had a visitor.'

'An early one, I'm afraid.' Brad rose to his feet and held out his hand. 'I'm Brad Lancing… You must be Steve.'

The two men shook hands. Neither smiled, and Steve's face had a cool, guarded look.

Joanne took a deep breath. 'Mr Lancing called to—'

'Brad, please… There's no need for formality outside the office.'

'Brad,' she tried not to stumble over the name, 'called because he's in need of a secretary…'

As she paused momentarily, searching for the right words, Steve said, 'Well, as Milly's in Scotland, I fail to see how—'

Hearing the faint suggestion of antagonism in her

brother's tone, Joanne broke in hastily, 'You don't understand… Somehow there's been a mix-up—'

'What kind of a mix-up?'

'Milly failed to hand in her notice, and apparently no
one realised she was leaving so soon. Brad is going to
Norway today, and, as there's no other secretary available,
I've agreed to go in Milly's place,' she finished in a rush.

Looking taken aback, Steve demanded, 'What about your
own job?'

'Lisa could take over for the few weeks I'll be away.
She said only yesterday that she didn't have enough to do.'

Seeing by Steve's face that he was about to argue, Joanne
said decidedly, 'I'm sure she'd jump at the chance to get
some added experience. And, as Milly has let Brad down,
I feel I owe it to him.'

'I don't see that it's *your* responsibility to make up for
Milly's misunderstanding.'

'Perhaps not.' Then knowing she had to convince him it
was what she *wanted* to do, she added, 'But I'd very much
like the chance to see something of Norway.'

'I can't imagine your *fiancé* will care for the idea of you
being away so long.' It was obvious that Steve had em-
phasised the relationship for Brad's benefit.

With more confidence than she felt, she said, 'He'll understand when I explain about Milly.'

'You're going to ring him?'

'Yes.'

She would have to make time to break the news. Trevor
was already seriously displeased with her over the concert
tickets, and this *desertion*, as he would no doubt see it,
certainly wouldn't help matters…

Feeling too stressed at the moment to cope with what
she felt sure would be an angry and hostile reaction, she
chickened out. 'But not now. He's taking his mother to
Bournemouth for the weekend. When I'm sure he's back
I'll decide on the best way to break it to him.'

'Well, of course, it's up to you,' Steve said with obvious disapproval. 'How soon will you have to start for the airport?'

'As soon as possible.' It was Brad who answered. 'There's a lunch-time flight from Heathrow to Bergen via Oslo.'

'You'll be based in Bergen?'

'Yes. I'll give you the address and phone number.' Then to Joanne, 'You won't have had breakfast yet, but we'll get something to eat at the airport.'

She nodded, and rose to her feet.

'How long will it take you to pack and get ready?'

'Half an hour or so. I can't say exactly,' she answered shortly.

Catching his eye, and suddenly daunted by the gleam of anger she saw there, she added, 'But I'll be as quick as I can.' Then was annoyed with herself.

'Two things... Don't forget your passport...'

Seeing what might be a way out, she was about to say she hadn't got one, when she recalled telling him about the trip to Amsterdam. Sighing inwardly, she wished she had kept her mouth shut. But it was too late now.

'And do pack a raincoat.'

Rattled, because it sounded like an order, she asked sweetly, 'What about gumboots?'

'Good idea,' he answered, straight-faced. 'It can be very wet in Bergen.'

Bested, she made a rapid retreat.

Steve followed her into the hall and, his blue eyes worried, said urgently, 'I just hope you know what you're doing.'

'At my age I should do,' she answered levelly.

'Look, Jo, I'm well aware that you're no silly schoolgirl, but you will watch your step, won't you? Brad Lancing has—'

'If you're going to say a wife—' she began.

'I'm not. It appears my informant was mixing him up with his cousin, *Blake* Lancing, who works for the firm, and who *has* got a wife and family...

'But what I intended to say when you interrupted me was, Brad Lancing has loads of sex appeal and, where women are concerned, apparently, not too many scruples.'

'So?'

Looking uncomfortable, Steve came to the point. 'Though I wouldn't have thought you were his type, he may have designs on you...'

Joanne was smiling a little at the old-fashioned phrase, when he added, 'And in some respects you're more naïve and vulnerable than Milly, and less able to take care of yourself.'

'Thanks a lot,' she said wryly.

'Listen to me, Sis,' Steve persisted. 'Lancing's a wealthy, sophisticated man, way out of your league. He's a heart-breaker, with a reputation for loving 'em and leaving 'em—'

'Don't worry, I know all about his reputation,' she interrupted firmly.

'And you still intend to go?'

'Yes.'

Steve sighed. 'I just don't want you to get badly hurt.'

'I won't.'

He looked unconvinced.

'Don't worry about me.' She gave him a hug. 'I'll leave you to explain things to Lisa. But I'll make the time to have a quick word with Milly before I go.'

Looking surprised, he said, 'In view of her crush on Lancing, I didn't think you'd want to tell her.'

'I've no intention of telling her, but if I don't get in touch to make sure they've arrived safely she might ring after I've gone.'

'Yes, I see what you mean.'

'If I can keep her in ignorance for the time being, all

well and good. Knowing Milly, she'll want to set about redecorating the new flat, so for the foreseeable future she's likely to be wrapped up in her own affairs.'

'Well, if she does ask where you are we'll stall her and let you know, then you can give her a ring...'

'Hang on, we're forgetting something. What about your birthday?'

'Oh, no,' Joanne groaned. 'She's sure to get in touch for that... Well, if at all possible, I'd like you to hide the fact that I've gone to Norway with Brad. I should hate to unsettle her.'

'Tell you what, I'll swear blind you've gone to Paris with Trevor.'

He turned to go back to the kitchen as his sister hurried up the stairs.

When Joanne had showered and dressed in a smart suit and a white tailored blouse, and taken her hair into a neat coil, she set about unearthing her case from the depths of the built-in wardrobe.

Steadfastly refusing to think about what lay ahead, she packed as quickly as possible, putting in only what she considered to be essentials.

As she closed the lid and fastened it she noticed Trevor's ring, and wondered, Would it be best to leave it at home?

But if she took it off Brad might get the wrong idea. No, she would keep it on and hope that it might act as some kind of safeguard.

Though, since she knew the kind of man he was, that could well be a vain hope.

Gathering up her belongings, she carried her case downstairs and stood it in the hall while she rang Milly, who answered with a grudging, 'Hello?'

'Hi! So you're home?'

'Oh, it's you! I thought it was another patient. We've

had two calls already and the surgery doesn't open until nine.'

Deciding to ignore that, Joanne asked, 'Did you have a good journey?'

'Very good. Slept the whole way, and the train got in on time. There's a supermarket just round the corner from here, so we did a quick shop and were in the flat before eight-thirty.'

'What's it like?'

'Quite spacious and not badly furnished, but most of the walls are a boring beige, which means one of our first jobs will be to redecorate.

'Most of the boxes we sent ahead have already arrived and are waiting to be unpacked, so we've an awful lot of work to do before we can get properly settled. I hate unpacking! I'm at the stage where I can't find a thing…'

As Joanne listened to a string of complaints both the men appeared in the hall. Steve, usually one of the most even-tempered of people, was looking more than a little flushed and aggressive, while Brad appeared to be as cool as a proverbial cucumber. She wondered what they had been saying to each other.

'At the moment,' Milly was going on, 'the kettle seems to be missing, which is a dratted nuisance…'

'Well, I'd better let you get on and look for it.' Joanne made her voice as cheerful as possible. 'I'll be in touch before too long to—'

'Jo,' Milly broke in, 'has Brad been in touch?'

'No, he hasn't,' Joanne lied hardly, and, meeting those green eyes, saw by the mockery in them that he knew quite well what question she'd been answering.

Biting her lip, she added quickly, 'Here's Steve to have a word. Take care, now. Love to Duncan.'

As she handed the receiver to her brother he gave her a one-armed hug, and whispered, 'If you need rescuing, just let me know.'

Brad picked up her case and, like a programmed robot, she led the way to the door. On the threshold, she turned to blow Steve a kiss.

The morning was clear and sunny, and as they descended the steps a playful breeze snatched a handful of bright leaves from a silver birch and swirled them around their heads like confetti.

They could be a couple leaving on their honeymoon, she thought with bitter irony.

While the chauffeur stowed her case, Brad helped her into the limousine and, taking a seat by her side, regarded her quizzically.

Running a finger beneath the lapel of her smart charcoal-grey business suit, he asked, 'Do you always dress to make a statement?'

She answered primly, without looking at him, 'I try to wear what's suitable for the occasion.'

'Then I shall certainly look forward to tonight.'

Suppressing a shudder, she moved as far away from him as possible, and the journey to the airport continued without another word being spoken.

While the silence stretched Joanne went back over the last hour or so, trying to come to terms with the appalling situation she found herself in; trying to find some way of escape.

Without success.

In spite of racking her brains, she could find no solution. It seemed she would be forced to go through with it. But how exactly was she going to play the hand her own stupidity had landed her with?

She considered briefly whether she could refuse to have any social contact. If she just did her job, carried out orders, spoke to him as little as possible and then only about business...

But common sense told her that wouldn't help matters.

In fact, being difficult, while it might give her a certain satisfaction, could only make a bad situation worse.

After all, if she shared his meals and his evenings, listened when he wanted to talk, appeared to conform, it didn't mean she had surrendered.

If she remained coolly polite, and acted in a civilised manner, as though he was simply her employer, it might make things more bearable.

And if he *had* intended to force her to share his bed, he might change his mind and find someone else.

As Steve had pointed out, Brad Lancing was a man with loads of sex appeal. There must be plenty of women who would be only too delighted to be his sleeping partner. So was there anything to be gained by trying to coerce an unwilling one?

He had no real interest in *her*. She was far from beautiful, not at all the kind of woman to attract a man like him. The only thing he wanted was revenge.

Don't get mad, get even.

Remembering his words, the confidence she had been trying to build began to crumble away.

But somehow, whatever happened, she would have to cope. And the only way she could do that was to refuse to think ahead. She must ignore what *might* happen, and find some means of getting through the here and now relatively unscathed…

Having thought it through, and made her decision, Joanne felt a little more settled by the time they reached the busy airport.

While the chauffeur dealt with the luggage she accompanied Brad to the desk to check in for their flight with something approaching equanimity.

Formalities completed, he said, 'We've got about an hour before our flight will be called, so I suggest we go and have something to eat.'

'How long will the journey take?' she asked as he led

her through the bustling throng of people to the nearest restaurant.

'The flight to Oslo takes about an hour and three quarters, and that's followed by a short hop across country to Bergen.

'Norwegian time is an hour ahead of ours, so, taking everything into account, we should arrive just nicely for dinner.'

As soon as they were seated and had each scanned the menu a waiter appeared at their table with a pad and pencil.

Turning to Joanne, Brad suggested, 'Though it's closer to lunch time than breakfast, what about bacon and eggs and all the trimmings?'

Finding she was suddenly ravenously hungry, she agreed, 'That sounds fine,' and caught his look of surprise.

As the waiter whisked away, without thinking she asked, 'Were you expecting me to go on hunger strike?'

His eyes, a clear dark green with very black pupils, looked amused. 'No, but I noticed you ate very little last night.'

'I wasn't hungry then.' She had been so intent on playing her part, and there had been so much adrenaline pumping into her bloodstream, that she hadn't wanted to eat.

'It occurred to me that you might be one of those tiresome women who prefer to live on raw carrots and lettuce leaves.'

'Before too long you might wish I was.'

He raised an enquiring brow. 'Why's that?'

'If I feel stressed I tend to eat more, and, as you'll presumably be paying for my food…'

He laughed, and she noted again that his mouth and teeth were excellent. 'I think the budget will stand it.' Slyly, he added, 'And it's a well-known fact that certain…shall we say…*activities* burn up quite a large number of calories.'

Watching her cheeks turn the colour of poppies, he went on with smooth satisfaction, 'So we'll have to make sure you get plenty of exercise. What would your brother think if I took you home all roly poly?'

Knowing that if she let herself be thrown by his teasing she would only be playing into his hands, she fought back. 'That's unlikely. Even without…exercise, I have the kind of metabolism that burns off fat…'

She saw a gleam of admiration in his eyes as she added, 'Steve is the same. Whereas Milly—'

'Can't look at a biscuit without putting on weight? Yes, she mentioned it… And before you get all indignant, it was a casual remark made at the office during a coffee break.'

At that moment their breakfast arrived.

'All the trimmings' included fresh orange juice, toast and marmalade, and a large pot of coffee.

As they tucked in Brad observed, 'I noticed that you and your brother are very alike physically… And I strongly suspect in character as well.'

He added the rider with a dryness that made her ask sharply, 'Why do you say that?'

A glint in his eye, he asked, 'Why do you think?'

Remembering how she'd smacked his face, a look of horror dawning, she whispered, 'He didn't…?'

'No, he didn't. But I got the impression he would have liked to take me on. Judging by what he said, he seems to share your very poor opinion of me…'

Her heart sank. Steve, with no idea what harm this man could do to him—and to his business.

Brad's smile was grim. 'And, though he managed to stay quiet and relatively civil, he warned me off in no uncertain terms.

'Having pointed out, yet again, that you were engaged to be married, he added that if I laid so much as a finger on you I'd have him to reckon with.

'He seems to think that you're sweet and inexperienced and might be in danger of losing your girlish innocence—'

'You didn't tell him the truth?' she broke in anxiously.

'What? That you've had *lots* of experience? No, I thought it might shock him.'

She bit her lip. 'You know what I mean. That you'd coerced me into coming... I don't want him to worry.'

'His only worry is that you might be vulnerable, and in danger of not only losing your fiancé, but also falling in love with me. If he'd known you hated the sight of me and...' Breaking off, he queried, 'I take it you *do* hate the sight of me?'

'What do you think?'

Laughing at her vehemence, he went on, 'And had only agreed to accompany me under duress he would have consigned me to hell-blazing rather than let you come. I must say, I admired his guts.'

'He cares about me,' she said simply.

Their journey proved to be pleasant and uneventful, and, tired from her virtually sleepless night, Joanne slept for most of the first part and dozed for the second, Brad only wakening her as they began their descent.

They came in to land at Flesland Airport through low cloud and rain.

'Though it's usually mild on the coast, it's wet for over two hundred days in the year,' Brad told her. 'Luckily the weather seldom seems to spoil the lovely views.'

As soon as the formalities were over they collected their luggage and made their way to the exit. Outside the air was warm and shrouded with mist and gentle rain.

There was a taxi rank close by, and as an empty vehicle drew up Brad handed their cases to the driver and, having given the man directions in fluent Norwegian, helped her in.

Joanne was vaguely surprised that no car was waiting for him. She would have expected the firm to have sent one.

As though reading her mind, he said, 'I wanted to keep

our arrival a secret until I've had time to talk to Paul Randall and assess the situation.'

'It all sounds very cloak-and-daggerish,' she remarked.

'You could say that,' he agreed lightly.

When he made no attempt to elaborate, after a moment or two she changed the subject. 'I don't like to appear terribly ignorant, but where exactly *is* the airport?'

'About twelve miles south of Bergen. When there's not a lot of traffic it takes somewhere in the region of thirty minutes to drive into the centre of town.

'It's a great pity there was so much low cloud today, otherwise you would have had a good view from the air.

'Bergen is known as "the city of the seven hills" because, as well as being beautifully situated on the coast, it's enfolded at the crook of seven mountains and fishboned by seven fjords...'

Driving on the right, their windscreen wipers steady as a metronome, they left the airport along with a fair number of other vehicles, including the *Flybussen*, which Brad translated as the airport bus.

Rain virtually obscured the view from the taxi windows, isolating them, cutting them off from the rest of the traffic and the outside world.

She was suddenly very aware of him, of how close he was sitting, and the fact that his thigh was almost brushing hers. Finding the intimacy overpowering, but unwilling to admit it, she tried surreptitiously to inch away.

The corner of his long mouth twitched, convincing her that he had noticed and been amused by her manoeuvre.

Flustered, needing something to say, she asked, 'Where are we staying?'

'There are plenty of good, modern hotels, but I thought we'd stay at Lofoten.'

'Lofoten?' she echoed uncertainly.

'The house my mother was born in. It's not far from the centre of town, and within walking distance of the harbour

and the offices. That being the case, I decided it would
make as suitable a base as any.

'Lofoten's a large place, and it needed to be, as my great-
great-great grandparents had numerous offspring, quite a
few of whom ended up in Chicago.

'After my grandfather's death, as I didn't want to part
with the house, and there was no point in letting it stand
empty, it was turned into a small hotel...'

Slanting her a glance, he queried mockingly, 'Relieved?'

'Yes,' she said boldly. And she was. For an uncomfortable minute she had visualised being quite alone with him.
At least in a hotel there would be other people close by.

CHAPTER FOUR

ONCE past the electronic-toll inner ring road that surrounded downtown Bergen they drove through the modern part of the town and were soon in the centre.

Peering through the rain-misted taxi window, Joanne saw that most of it appeared to be old and historic.

As they crossed the end of the long, narrow harbour Brad said, 'This is Torget, Bergen's market-place. It's also known as Fisketorget.

'At the turn of the last century fishermen in wellington boots and women in long aprons used to gut the fish catch here.'

Beyond a sprawl of crooked streets lined with a hotchpotch of picturesque architecture that seemed to house a plethora of antiques shops they came to a slightly more open area.

'Here we are,' Brad said as the taxi drew up in front of an old and rambling two-storey wooden building. Standing on the edge of what appeared to be spacious walled grounds, it was painted red-ochre, and had long, small-paned windows, arched at the top.

'This has been the family home for several hundred years,' he told her, a note of quiet pride in his voice. 'The fabric itself hasn't altered much, though the house has seen quite a few changes in its time.'

Set back from the road with a smoothly pebbled frontage brightened by tubs of late-summer flowers, it was sturdily built of clapboard, with ornate shingles and overhanging eaves. A board above the entrance porch said simply, 'Lofoten.'

Standing on the narrow pavement in the gentle rain,

while Brad paid the driver and dealt with their luggage, Joanne stared up at the roof-ridge, fascinated by the family of carved, intertwined dragon-like creatures that cavorted there.

Noticing her absorption, he asked, 'Like the Lofoten dragons?'

Turning to him, she breathed, 'They're wonderful. They have so much character.' Pointing, she added, 'Look at the expression on that little one's face, he looks quite pained.'

'Can you see why?'

Returning her attention to the roof, she laughed. 'Yes! That big one's standing on his tail.'

Gazing into her glowing face, where moisture beaded her eyebrows and long lashes and a drop of water trickled down her cheek, Brad thought in surprise, *Why, she's beautiful,* and had to subdue a sudden impulse to kiss her.

Showing no sign of tearing herself away, despite the softly falling rain, she exclaimed, 'Oh, just look at the baby!'

'I agree, he's delightful,' Brad said drily. 'But, on a strictly practical note, your hair's wet now, and if we stand here much longer we'll both be soaked to the skin...

'Though, on the plus side, we could always share a hot tub, then have the pleasure of rubbing each other down...'

Galvanised by his rider, she reached the porch ahead of him.

Making no attempt to hide his grin, he suggested, 'If you'd be kind enough to release the door catch?'

Wondering crossly how he could so easily destroy her composure, rattle the cool, level-headed woman she had prided herself on being, she obeyed.

He shouldered open the heavy door and led the way into a large foyer, deserted except for a woman at the reception desk.

The floor, ceiling, and walls were all of old smoky-gold

wood. In the centre a handsomely carved staircase led up
to a balustraded landing.

Used as she was to carpets and floor coverings, Joanne's
first impression was of rustic simplicity and a certain austereness. Yet at the same time there was an air of homeli-
ness, of welcome, which was largely engendered by a
green-and-blue tiled stove shaped like a giant beehive that
threw out a glowing warmth.

In front of the stove was a jewel-bright woven mat that
matched the curtains at the windows, a leather settee and
several chairs the colour of maple syrup, and a sturdy little
coffee-table. To one side was an alcove stacked high with
logs that smelled of pine.

Looking up from a computer screen, the fair-haired
woman at the reception desk smiled a greeting, and said in
excellent English, 'Mr Lancing...how very nice to see you!
What a pity it is raining.'

He put the cases down and, returning her smile, asked,
'How are you, Helga?'

'I am very well. I hope it is the same with you?'

'Indeed it is.' An arm around Joanne's waist, he drew
her forward. 'This is Miss Winslow.'

He hadn't said *my secretary*.

Glancing at Joanne's engagement ring speculatively,
Helga said, 'It is nice to meet you, Miss Winslow.' Again
there was that friendly smile.

Joanne managed to smile back.

'I'm sorry it was such short notice,' Brad said.

'Your suite is always kept ready for you,' Helga assured
him, 'so it is not a problem. I will call Edvard to deal with
your cases.'

'Don't bother, I'll take them.'

He turned to Joanne and, an unmistakable challenge in
those green eyes, asked, 'Ready, darling?'

Since deciding at the start of the journey how to play her

hand she had gone through the motions like an actress forced to audition for a role she neither liked nor wanted.

Now the journey was over, they had arrived, and suddenly this was no longer just a role she could back out of, it was all too real. But for everyone's sake she *had* to go through with it…

Somehow she forced her unwilling legs to follow him as he led the way over to the small lift. The cases taking up quite a lot of floor space, they stood very close together as, creaking and wheezing asthmatically, the lift climbed to the next floor.

When they reached the landing Brad turned left down a passageway and, dropping one of the cases briefly, opened the door at the end and ushered her into a living-room.

It was comfortably furnished and homely, with a huge leather couch, two armchairs, a television and stereo, a grandmother clock, and a series of well-stocked bookcases.

Situated between the windows was a fireplace and in it, complementing the central heating, a tiled stove, a smaller version of the one in the lobby. To each side was a stack of logs, and in front of it a thick white goatskin rug.

A door to the left opened into a room with a desk and an array of expensive computer equipment. Another door led into the bathroom.

Putting down his own case, Brad told her casually, 'As you might guess, this was originally a second bedroom, but I decided it would be a lot more useful as an office.'

Joanne's heart sank like a stone. Until that minute she had been clinging to the faint hope that she might have a room of her own.

Perhaps it was the fact that there was only one bedroom that had made him avoid introducing her as his secretary. Calling her simply Miss Winslow had allowed Helga to draw her own conclusions.

He opened a door to the right and, his eyes on her face,

as though to gauge her reaction, added, 'However, this is plenty big enough for both of us.'

Putting her case on a low chest, he continued conversationally, 'I originally chose rooms at the rear of the house because it's quieter, and the view, when you can see it, is better.'

The *en suite* bedroom, with windows looking out over a terrace and what appeared to be a fairly extensive garden, was airy and pleasant. It had light, modern furniture, two walk-in wardrobes and a king-sized bed topped by a sumptuous-looking duvet.

Her thoughts suddenly focused on the coming night, Joanne found herself staring at the bed, mesmerised, unable to look away.

She could visualise Brad joining her there. Naked. Instinctively she knew that he wouldn't wear pyjamas. He would have a good body, firm and muscular. His hands—until then she hadn't realised she had noticed his hands—were strong and well-shaped with long fingers and neatly trimmed nails. Skilful hands, no doubt…

Erotic images began to form in her mind, sending heat surging through her entire body. A heat that, she was horrified to realise, wasn't caused totally by dread and aversion, but held an unwelcome measure of excitement.

Noting that her eyes were fixed on the bed, with no change of tone he asked, 'Which side do you prefer?'

She stiffened and forced herself to look away. 'I prefer to sleep alone.'

'Always?'

'Always.'

'What about Trevor?'

'Trevor isn't the kind of man who…' She broke off. Knowing that she'd already broken the news to Trevor—she'd said no! Joanne shivered as a drop of cold water ran from the dark hair at her nape and trickled down her neck.

Seeing that shiver, he said, 'You can tell me about Trevor later. At the moment you need to dry your hair.'

She had intended to wash it this morning… But 'this morning' now seemed to belong in another life.

'I'd like to take a shower.' She spoke the thought aloud.

A devilish glint in his eye, he asked, 'Feel like sharing one?'

'No, I don't. I agreed to be your secretary, not your mistress!'

'Pity. Still, it's early days yet. When you get to know me better—'

'I still won't want you!'

Seeing his grin, she wished she'd ignored him instead of rising to the bait.

Glancing though the window, he observed, 'The rain seems to be easing off and the clouds are lifting, which means a fine evening. If you like, I'll book a table and we'll have dinner out and do a spot of sightseeing.'

'That would be nice,' she agreed politely.

He ran lean fingers over his chin. 'I'll need to shave, and I've a few things to set up. I also want a quick word with Paul Randall.

'People tend to eat fairly early here, so shall we say about an hour?'

She nodded.

His hand on the latch, he turned. 'By the way, there's no need to dress up. Something pretty and informal will do fine…'

Though it was politely phrased, she recognised it as an order.

'And it might be as well if you bring a jacket in case it turns cool later on.'

When the door had closed behind him she took off her suit and tailored blouse, and opened her case to find her wash bag.

It was just as well he didn't want her to dress up, she

thought wryly, surveying the clothes she had packed. She hadn't a thing that was really dressy with her.

Apart from another business suit, a raincoat, a fleece, some woollies, and a designer jacket she'd pushed in on impulse, she had nothing but jeans, skirts and tops.

She might just as well stick with what she had been wearing.

Going through to the surprisingly luxurious bathroom, she pushed home the small bolt—just to be on the safe side—and, trying to keep her mind fixed on the immediate future, stepped into the shower cubicle.

But as she showered and shampooed her hair, try as she might, her recalcitrant thoughts kept straying to the coming night with a combination of dread and fascination.

What on earth was the matter with her? she wondered irritably. This was so out of character, so *unlike* her.

Even when she was younger, unlike a lot of her friends, she had felt no impulse to dabble, to experience for herself what she had been led to believe was a potentially explosive force. Several of the older boys had tried to interest her but, rather than be attracted by their sweaty hands and hot mouths, she had been repelled.

And as she got older she had been unable to respond in the way her boyfriends wanted, and she had come to the conclusion that some vital spark was missing from her make-up.

Tired of being tried and found wanting, she had avoided serious petting. Then after the death of her parents she had had no time for a social life.

Deciding regretfully that she probably wasn't destined to have a husband and children, she had settled on a career.

Then, at the beginning of the year, a business acquaintance had introduced her to Trevor Wilky, and a steady, low-key relationship had developed that had given her cause to think again about her future.

But what this nightmare she was caught up in would do to that relationship she dared not begin to think…

Sighing, she turned off the water and, stepping from the scented shower-stall, reached for a towel to wrap turban-wise around her head while she dried herself and pulled on a bathrobe.

Amongst the bathroom's plush fittings were a cream hair-dryer and a styling-brush.

Wondering if they had been installed for the women Brad brought here, she dried her hair, pulled her own brush through it, and took it up into its usual neat, shining coil. Then, going through to the bedroom, she put on fresh un-dies, and the suit and blouse she had taken off earlier.

With a clear, creamy skin and well-marked brows and lashes, she needed very little in the way of make-up. A dab of compressed powder to stop her nose shining, a hint of blue eye-shadow, a touch of lip-gloss, and she was ready.

Picking up her shoulder bag, she ventured into the living-room. At first she could see no sign of Brad, then through the half-open door of his office she glimpsed him at his desk, his dark head bent over some papers.

The heels of her neat court shoes were rubber-tipped and made no sound, but as though sensing her presence he glanced up.

Leaving what he was doing, he rose to his feet and joined her in the living-room. Freshly shaven, his hair still a little damp from the shower, he had changed from his suit into smart-casual clothes, and looked relaxed and handsome.

His gaze swept over her from head to toe and back again in silence, taking in her suit and blouse and her businesslike hairdo.

His chiselled lips tightened and, meeting his eyes she read the displeasure in their cool green depths.

'You said there was no need to dress up,' she reminded him defensively.

'That's true,' he agreed, his tone even. 'But I also specified something pretty and informal. The suit you're wearing is neither.'

'Well, I'm afraid it will have to do,' she said coldly.

She saw the displeasure turn to anger.

'While ideal for business, it could hardly be described as appropriate for an evening out. Everyone will think you're my secretary.'

Scared of his anger, and despising herself for being scared, she said, 'I am.'

'Only when we're at the office. At all other times you will please dress as though you were fulfilling the other half of your brief.'

Angry in her turn, she said shortly, 'I'm afraid I don't have anything tarty enough for a mistress.'

'Then we'll need to do some shopping. In the meantime, I'd like you to take off the things you're wearing and change into something more suitable for dining out.'

Standing her ground, she said, 'I've no intention of taking them off…'

Her words ended in a gasp as, disposing of her handbag and jacket, with great deliberation he began to undo the buttons of her blouse.

His fingers brushed against her breasts, and, trying to push his hands away, she gasped, 'What are you doing?'

'Taking them off for you.'

In desperation she insisted, 'But I haven't *got* anything more suitable…'

He finished undoing the buttons, and in spite of her resistance began to tug the blouse free from the waistband of her skirt.

'In that case, we'll stay in after all. I'll have a meal sent up, and we'll think of something else to do to pass the evening.'

Scared stiff of what that 'something else' might be, she assured him shakily, 'It's the truth… You can come and look for yourself if you don't believe me.'

Dragging the edges of her blouse together, she led the way into the bedroom, and threw open the lid of her case.

He had a quick rifle through it and, selecting a silky skirt patterned in brown and rust, a cream top with a cowl neckline, a pair of strappy sandals and her fun-fur designer jacket, said coolly, 'These are fine. Now, do you need any help to get into them?'

'No, I don't—and I'm only changing to shut you up!'

'Then I'll leave you to it.'

With shaking hands she took off what she was wearing and dressed in what he had chosen, while admitting she had been silly to oppose him.

Such opposition got her nowhere, and only made things worse. If she could only tell him to go to hell and walk out. But for Steve's sake, she couldn't. Brad was the master. He held the whip and was quite prepared to crack it.

As soon as she was ready she picked up her jacket and reluctantly returned to the living-room.

He was standing with his back to her, looking out over the dusky garden, apparently deep in thought.

Pausing, she noticed afresh how broad his shoulders were in comparison to his hips, how symmetrical and supple the line of his spine.

She knew by now that he was light on his feet, easy and graceful, yet carrying with him an air of authority, a self-confidence that amounted almost to arrogance.

Joanne sighed. Her mother would have undoubtedly classed him as a man's man and a woman's darling.

There was no denying he was a superb male animal, and the fact that she couldn't fault him physically only made her hate him more.

He turned at her approach, and nodded his approval. 'A great improvement.'

'I'm so glad you think so,' she said with saccharine-sweetness.

The glint that appeared in his eye made her wish she could learn not to provoke him.

'There's just one more thing…' He moved towards her, and suddenly he was much too close for comfort.

Before she could begin to guess his intention he spun her round and began to deftly remove the pins from her hair.

As the thick, silky mass came cascading around her shoulders he remarked with satisfaction, 'That's better.'

Tossing the pins aside, he turned her to face him and, holding her upper arms, stood looking down steadily into her stormy eyes.

Only when her gaze fell beneath his did he add, 'I much prefer your hair loose. It makes you look a great deal more feminine.

'And I do like my women to look feminine.'

Such a masculine man would, she thought, while bitterly resenting the way he had phrased it.

'Now, if you're ready to go?'

Biting her lip, she allowed herself to be helped into the fun-fur jacket and escorted down the stairs and across a lobby now lit by hanging lamps.

It was no longer deserted. A party of new arrivals clustered round the desk, and an elderly couple sat in front of the glowing stove drinking coffee.

When they got outside it was to find the evening was clear and dry and comparatively mild. Only the still-damp pavements showed it had been raining.

Tucking her hand through his arm, Brad said, 'I thought a stroll as far as the Rosenkrantz Tower, to stretch our legs, then dinner on Bryggen.'

'Bryggen?'

'The quay. An historic place. The buildings there are on the World Heritage list. They also form a major tourist attraction, and house boutiques, museums and restaurants.'

As the dusk thickened lights began to spring up everywhere. Traffic was busy and bustling, and laughing groups of people thronged the pavements, looking all set to paint the town.

'Is there much nightlife?' Joanne asked as they walked.

'Quite a lot. Most of it's in the centre, and at weekends the harbour area in particular tends to get crowded.'

'Nightclubs, that sort of thing?'

'There's everything from piano bars to discos, as well as the kind of cosy meeting place where you can go for a drink and find earnest students and the local intelligentsia.

'The piano bar at the Kirkenes is well worth a visit. I'll take you there tomorrow night…'

While she looked around her with unfeigned interest they walked until they got to the short and sturdy Rosenkrantz Tower.

Thinking it looked a bit like a folly, she asked, 'What was its purpose?'

'It was built in the middle of the fifteen-hundreds by Erik Rosenkrantz as a fortified official residence.'

Standing a few feet away, a camera slung around his neck, a balding tourist who had followed them there appeared to be listening with interest.

When Joanne had had time to admire the picturesque tower they turned and retraced their steps until they reached Ovregaten.

'Ovregaten forms the back boundary of Bryggen,' Brad told her. 'All these narrow passages are where the citizens of Bergen used to live in the fourteenth century.'

Glancing around while she listened, she noticed that the tourist, who had apparently followed them back, was once more listening.

'After several disastrous fires,' Brad went on, 'the surviving buildings on Bryggen are mostly reconstructions, the oldest dating from around seventeen hundred…'

He pointed out a row of wooden structures, whose gables

faced the harbour. Topped with triangular pastry-cutter roofs, they were painted red, blue, yellow and green.

The harbourside was illuminated, and the modest buildings, along with the stocky tower and the yachts lining the pier, were reflected in the still water.

'Isn't it wonderful?' she breathed.

'It's renowned for being one of the most beautiful cityscapes in Northern Europe.'

Hearing the quiet pride in his voice, she knew he loved his mother's homeland.

When they reached the restaurant Brad had chosen it proved to be an old timber building with crooked floors and a lively Wild-West-saloon-bar-type ambience.

They were greeted at the door, and Joanne was relieved of her jacket, before they were led to a secluded booth beneath a wooden balcony, and handed large menus.

'What a fascinating place,' she said as she settled herself on the bench.

'I thought you might like it.'

Catching sight of the balding tourist who had followed them to and from the Rosenkrantz Tower being turned away, she commented, 'It seems we were lucky to get a table.'

'I see our friend didn't.'

She was surprised by the satisfaction in his voice.

'At such short notice we wouldn't have if they hadn't known me,' he added.

'With two of the best chefs in town, and a traditional menu that features marinaded moose and roast reindeer, it's always booked well ahead by locals and tourists alike.'

When she remarked on the fact that a lot of the well-, but casually, dressed clientele were speaking English he explained, 'English is taught in the schools here, so a lot of Norwegians speak it fluently.'

After studying the menu she refused the more exotic dishes, and settled for grilled salmon and a fruit dessert.

While they sipped a cocktail and waited for their food to arrive, keeping to impersonal topics, they conversed with an ease that surprised her.

He was an intelligent and stimulating companion who, instead of talking down to her, as Trevor quite often did, treated her as his intellectual equal.

There was an interesting edge of irony and a certain dry humour to his observations that she found refreshing, and, without being in the least arbitrary, he had clear and well-formed views on most things.

Views that she could find no fault with. In fact, to her even greater surprise, she agreed with many of them.

Nor could she fault his behaviour.

There was nothing to be seen of the man who had set himself out to seduce Milly, the libertine who had run his hand up her thigh.

Correct and courteous, he was a charming host who showed not the slightest sign of overstepping the mark, and as the meal progressed she found herself in real danger of enjoying his company.

But a leopard didn't change its spots.

She was reminding herself what kind of man he really was, and how much she loathed and despised him, when he glanced up and caught her eye.

'I don't need to ask what you're thinking,' he remarked sardonically. 'You have a very expressive face.'

Cursing his perspicacity, she felt the betraying colour rise in her cheeks.

At that moment, to her very great relief, their coffee was brought and served.

But it seemed as if, suddenly, the whole mood of the evening had changed, and Joanne found herself wishing that the uncomfortable little incident had never taken place.

Gnawing at her bottom lip, she was wondering how to break the lengthening silence and get back on some kind of reasonable footing, when Brad said, 'You were going to tell me about your fiancé.'

With no particular wish to talk about Trevor, she tried to wriggle out of it. 'There's not much to tell… And I've no idea where to start.'

'You could start by telling me what he looks like.'

Brad's earlier easy manner had vanished as though it had never been, and there was a coolness to his voice that made it clear he was responding to her tacit animosity.

But, having caused this new and hostile mood, she would somehow have to cope with it.

Which meant fight, or surrender.

Unwilling to either take him on or surrender totally, she chose a middle course. Even then, as she might have expected, it proved to be a running battle, with her doing the running.

His eyes on her face, Brad pressed, 'Is he tall or short, fat or thin, dark or fair?'

'He's tall and fair and quite nice-looking.'

'Quite nice-looking… As striking as that!'

'Do you *have* to be so sarcastic?'

With a mirthless grin, he said, 'I'm afraid a lukewarm description like that brings out the worst in me. But do go on, and I'll try to restrain myself.'

Like hell you will! she thought. Stifling the urge to say it aloud, she asked, 'What exactly do you want to know?'

'To start with, how old is he?'

'Thirty-six.'

'So he's past the impetuous years of youth.'

Trevor was so admirably sober and steady that Joanne couldn't believe he had ever been impetuous.

When she said nothing, Brad queried, 'And you're what? Twenty-five? Eleven years is quite a big difference.'

Sounding defensive, she said, 'I'll be twenty-five in a few days' time. But in any case I've never considered that age matters.'

Changing tack, Brad asked, 'I take it Trevor's an only child?'

Flustered by the question, she asked, 'What makes you think that?'

'I got the impression that he's something of a mother's boy.'

'There are worse things to be,' she said icily. 'At least Trevor's decent and upright, which is more than you can say for *some* men.'

He let that go, and asked satirically, 'Apart from the fact that he's decent and upright, what makes him your Mr Right?'

'We share the same interests.'

'Which are?'

'Reading...music and the arts...the theatre in particular.'

'No sports or outdoor activities?'

'Trevor isn't the sporty type.'

'Doesn't he even watch sport on the television?'

'No.'

'What about you?'

'I don't watch it either.'

He acknowledged the retort with a glinting smile, before rephrasing the question. 'Do *you* indulge in any outdoor activities?'

'I enjoy hiking and swimming.'

'Do you like skiing?'

'I've never had the chance to try.'

'If you had the chance, would you take it?'

'Yes.'

'And leave Trevor at home?'

When she remained silent, he said, 'Tell me about his faults. One can't weigh up a person without knowing their faults.'

All in all, Trevor had few really bad faults. Apart from wanting to lord it a bit, and having a tendency to tell her how to run her life, he had proved to be the ideal man-friend.

The main criterion was, though pleasantly attentive, he neither pressured her to sleep with him, nor demanded the kind of response she knew herself to be incapable of.

Having what she guessed was a lower than average sex drive, he had appeared perfectly satisfied with companionship, and a few less-than-passionate kisses.

'He hasn't got…' about to say 'many serious faults', she changed it to '…any serious faults.'

'A veritable paragon.'

'I'm lucky to have him,' she said firmly.

'How long *have* you had him?'

'We met about seven months ago.'

Reaching across the table, Brad picked up her hand and moved the solitaire from side to side with his thumb. 'And you've been engaged, how long?'

She wondered briefly whether to tell him the truth, and decided against it. If he had a speck of decency left, the belief that she had a fiancé might serve as some kind of protection.

Removing her hand, she answered evasively, 'Not very long.'

'How long is "not very long"?'

'A couple of weeks.'

'Does his mother approve?'

'Yes, she does,' Joanne said shortly.

'Perhaps she thinks it's time he was safely married to a *nice* girl. It's just as well she doesn't know that you've led her darling boy astray.'

'I haven't done anything of the kind,' Joanne protested indignantly.

'Surely you and Trevor have slept together?'

Without considering what Brad would make of it, she answered truthfully, 'No, we haven't.'

'Not even when you went to Amsterdam?'

'No.' Half expecting Trevor to suggest a double room, she had been bracing herself to agree, when, in the end, he had booked two singles.

Watching her face, Brad asked drily, 'Why not? Don't tell me he didn't want to... Or did Mother come along to keep an eye on her boy?'

'No, she didn't!'

'So why didn't you sleep together?'

'Not everyone has the "let's jump into bed" mentality. Trevor is happy to wait until we're married.'

'Is he, now? And what about you? While you're waiting, are you getting your fun elsewhere?'

'No! I certainly am not!'

He shook his head pityingly. 'You must be terribly frustrated. No wonder you offered to take—er—Milly's place.'

Well, she'd walked right into that one, she thought grimly, and denied through gritted teeth, 'I didn't mean it.'

'So you said. But I really think, things being as they are, you might quite enjoy it... In fact, I'll make absolutely sure you do.'

A slow, suffocating heat filling her, she shuddered.

His head tilted a little to one side, he queried, 'Is that a shiver of anticipation?'

'No, it isn't,' she said thickly. 'It's a shudder of loathing.'

But she was shaken afresh to realise that wasn't altogether true.

Turning her head, she looked anywhere but at him.

He smiled ironically. 'With a face that mirrors your feelings and your every thought, I'm afraid you don't make a very good liar... And when you refuse to look at me, like now, I know it's because you daren't.'

CHAPTER FIVE

WHILE she was still struggling to regain her equilibrium he asked, 'As a matter of interest, when are you getting married?'

Somehow she managed to answer, 'We haven't yet set a date.'

'Ah, well, that kind of decision needs careful thought. There's no point in rushing into it.'

'I'm so glad you approve.'

He got his own back by touching a fingertip to her hot cheek, then pulling it away and blowing on it.

Watching her soft mouth tighten, he suggested, 'Why don't you tell me about the actual proposal? How long had you been expecting it? I gather women know these things.'

Having presumed that Trevor was a born bachelor, his proposal had come right out of the blue. Though in retrospect she realised that she should have at least *suspected* his reason for ordering champagne—as far as he was concerned, an unusual and reckless extravagance.

'I hadn't been expecting it.'

'A *surprise* proposal! And, I suppose, being the model of excellence he is, he found a bench in some rose garden and went down on one knee?'

'No, he didn't.'

His voice mocking, Brad said, 'If I ever decide to propose to someone I really ought to know how it's done. So tell me, what did he do…?'

Trevor had taken her to one of the best restaurants in London and, clearing his throat, begun rather pompously, 'We get on very well together, wouldn't you say?'

'Yes,' she had agreed, a little puzzled by his manner. 'What makes you ask?'

'I want us to get engaged.' Before she realised his intention, he had taken her hand and slipped a diamond solitaire onto her third finger.

Taken completely by surprise, she blurted out, 'What about your mother?'

'Mother approves.'

'Oh…' she said a bit blankly.

'I've got a good job. I could take care of you and give you everything you and our children might need.'

'Well, I…'

'From the way you get on with Cousin Jean's twins, I know you're fond of children.'

That wasn't strictly true. She wasn't fond of children *en masse*, but as individuals she found them interesting and, in most cases, lovable.

'You'd like a family, wouldn't you?'

'Yes, but I—'

'You see, Mother's decided it's high time I got married and gave her some grandchildren.'

Someone else she could rule.

Pushing away that uncharitable thought, Joanne said carefully, 'If you don't mind, I'd like to think about it.'

Hurt that she hadn't jumped at the chance—as his mother had assured him she would—Trevor said huffily, 'I really don't see what there is to think about.'

Not wishing to wound him in any way, she explained seriously, 'Before I commit myself I have to be sure I could be the sort of wife you need.'

His blue eyes complacent, he told her, 'Mother seems to think you're exactly what I need. She's satisfied that you're a girl with good morals. The kind that doesn't play around.'

Recognising that as the highest accolade, Joanne said, 'I'm flattered, really I am. All the same I want to be certain I'm doing the right thing before I say yes.'

With a touch of irony, she added, 'I should hate to let you, or your mother, down.'

Somewhat mollified, he agreed, 'I suppose it makes sense to be absolutely sure.' Then magnanimously, 'Very well, take whatever time you need…'

When she attempted to slip off the ring he stopped her. 'I went to a great deal of trouble to choose that particular ring…'

It was the safe, conventional choice she would have expected a man like Trevor to make.

'Mother was convinced you'd like it, and so was I…' He sounded as disappointed as a child whose gift was in danger of being spurned.

'I *do* like it,' she assured him. 'But it wouldn't be right to wear it until I've made up my mind…

'Suppose I decide not to marry you?'

Unable to seriously believe such a thing could happen, he said comfortably, 'I'm sure you won't…'

And he was probably quite right, she conceded. Common sense said she should agree. Where would she find another decent man who had Trevor's attributes? A man who suited her half as well as he did?

If she couldn't bring herself to marry him she might as well accept the fact that she would never have a husband and children…

'Now the ring's on your finger, promise me you'll wear it while you're making up your mind,' Trevor went on. 'We would be *so* disappointed if I had to take it back.'

'Very well, I promise,' she answered reluctantly.

He smiled, showing teeth that were white and even. His mother had once told her how long he'd had to wear braces to produce such a perfect result. 'Knowing you as I do, I have no doubt at all that you'll make me a perfect wife…'

But as far as Joanne was concerned, even at the end of the evening, defying common sense, a little niggle of doubt still lingered…

*   *   *

Getting no immediate response to his question, Brad pursued, 'Or perhaps *you* proposed to him?'

Knowing he was just needling her, she said stiffly, 'Trevor took me out to dinner and ordered champagne, then he produced a ring and asked me to marry him.'

'With a declaration of undying love, presumably?'

Suddenly chilled by the thought that love had never been mentioned, she lied, 'Of course.'

'And you love him?'

'Why else would I have agreed to marry him?'

He shrugged. 'That depends on whether you think love is important?'

'What do you think?' The question was a challenge.

He answered seriously, 'As a matter of fact I think it's *very* important. So long as the other necessary ingredients are present, love is the glue that sticks a marriage together.'

Amazed that a man like him should think that way, she asked, 'What do you regard as "the necessary ingredients"?'

'Shared interests, sexual compatibility, respect, a liking for each other's company.'

Unable to argue with that, she found herself saying, 'I think so too.'

'So, swept off your feet, you accepted?'

'Yes,' she retorted defiantly.

Brad passed lean fingers over his smoothly shaven chin and, his voice thoughtful, remarked, 'That's a somewhat different version to the one your sister gave me.'

Startled, Joanne demanded, 'What version did Milly give you?'

'She said that Trevor had proposed, but you hadn't given him an answer, and she was hoping that when you had had time to think it over you'd turn him down.

'If I remember rightly, she described him as a pompous git.'

Caught on the raw, Joanne retorted, 'Even that's better than being a lying hypocrite, and that's what you are.'

His firm mouth tightened, and a steely glint appeared in those clear dark-green eyes.

Refusing to be intimidated, she rushed on, 'Don't you remember saying that I was mistaken about your relationship with Milly? That as far as you were concerned she was simply a nice girl and an efficient secretary?'

'As a matter of fact I do.'

'Well, that hardly sounds like the kind of conversation any ordinary secretary would have with her boss.'

'I agree that it wouldn't be if it had happened in the office—'

'So presumably it was when you took her out to dinner?'

'I didn't "take her out to dinner".'

'She told me you'd taken her out to dinner *twice.*'

'They were business dinners,' Brad said, his voice even. 'Both times there was someone else present, which I think you'll agree hardly counts as a romantic tête-à-tête.'

'I really don't see why you needed a secretary—' Joanne began.

'The meetings had been instigated by a man I didn't altogether trust,' Brad broke in firmly. 'I decided to have a secretary along to take notes so that the next day he couldn't wriggle out of what had been said and promised.'

'Are you trying to tell me the kind of conversation you had with Milly went on in front of someone else?'

'On the second occasion my client was delayed, and while Miss Winslow and I waited we had a drink and talked. Apart from a bit of family gossip, that's all there was to it.'

He made it sound so reasonable, so *credible.*

But, recalling how, when she had asked Milly, 'You didn't go any further?' Milly had answered, 'No, I didn't. But from some of the things he said, and the way he looked at me, I know he wanted to,' Joanne felt a fresh surge of anger.

Watching her face, Brad commented, 'You obviously don't believe me.'

'No, I don't,' Joanne informed him hardly. 'Milly told me differently.'

'Well, as it appears to be your sister's word against mine, and I'm sure you trust her implicitly—'

'Yes, I do…'

But even as she spoke, a little demon of doubt reminded Joanne that Milly was, at times, prone to exaggeration. To occasionally seeing things as she *wanted* them to be, rather than as they really were. If she fancied herself in love with her boss, might she not have read more into the situation than was warranted?

For a moment Joanne wavered. Could she have been mistaken about Brad Lancing?

Then came the memory of the way he had run his hand up her thigh, and her face hardened in condemnation. No, she wasn't mistaken. She knew from her own experience just what kind of man he was…

'Then perhaps we should change the subject.' Brad sounded resigned, almost bored.

'Perhaps we should,' she agreed icily.

'Tell me,' he resumed after a moment, 'how do you think Trevor will react to the idea of his fiancée running off without a word as soon as his back is turned…?

'You did say he'd taken his mother to Bournemouth?'

Ignoring the last provocative question, she said, 'It won't be without a word. I have every intention of phoning him after the weekend.'

'Suppose he takes it into his head to ring you at home tomorrow?'

'If he does, I'm sure Steve will explain.'

Only, knowing Trevor, he wouldn't ring.

On the rare occasions they had had a minor difference

of opinion, unable to believe he could be in the wrong, he had always left it to her to make the first move.

This time, unfortunately, the difference of opinion had developed into a major incident. When she had refused to go to the concert with him he had accused her of caring more for Milly than she did for him.

Finding he couldn't move her, he had been at first petulant, then downright angry. 'Why do you keep on mothering her, giving up everything for her? I know it's her last night at home, but you don't have to be there. She doesn't need you any longer. She's a married woman now, not a child...'

In spite of all her efforts to smooth things over, it had ended in what his mother was pleased to call 'a little fall-out'.

'In any case, I'll talk to him on Monday,' she added flatly.

'So what will you tell him? The whole truth?'

Horrified, she cried, 'No, of course not.'

'I thought you said he wasn't the jealous type?'

'He isn't... But for everyone's sake I want him to believe it's strictly business.'

'Even if he believes that, won't he be concerned that you're spending six weeks in Norway with a man who— according to you and your brother—has a bad reputation as far as women are concerned?'

'Yes, he might be.'

'Only *might*?'

'He trusts me.'

'Then all I can say is, he's a fool.'

'How dare you suggest...' Suddenly remembering the previous night, the way she had acted, she broke off abruptly, colour flooding into her face.

'Exactly,' Brad said softly.

'But I'm not really like that...' she blurted out. 'I was just trying to...'

'Tease?' he suggested when she hesitated.

'Protect Milly.'

'Are you quite sure Milly needs protecting?'

'When there are unscrupulous men like you around, yes, she does.'

'Funny, but she didn't strike me that way at all. In fact, I got the distinct impression that she's quite capable of taking care of herself. Maybe more so than you are.'

It stuck Joanne that Steve, who knew them both a great deal better, had said much the same thing.

'Most of the "experienced" women I've known,' Brad went on thoughtfully, 'have been sophisticated and hard as nails. Well able to take care of themselves. Or else the kind of girl one could only describe as weak, or promiscuous... In my opinion you're none of those things. Which I find distinctly intriguing...

'I'd also be fascinated to know why a girl who admits to having had lots of experience should choose to marry a man with no red blood in his veins.'

Watching her face, he smiled a little. 'Unless, of course, you lied about being experienced, and are really afraid of sex...'

Before she could find her voice, he added, 'Later, when we go to bed, no doubt I'll be able to solve the mystery.'

As she listened to his words that strange, tumultuous excitement she'd experienced earlier, and which had been lurking at some subconscious level in her mind, surfaced. Her breathing quickened and her heart began to throw itself against her ribs, while every nerve in her body sprang into life.

Brad stopped speaking and glanced up as a small party passed on their way to the door.

While they had been talking the restaurant had steadily emptied until now they were one of only two couples remaining.

'Are you about ready to go?' he queried politely.

'Yes, quite ready.' Though the words were positive enough, her voice shook a little.

'Then I think it's time we were moving.'

He signalled the waiter, and paid the bill, before rising to pull back her chair.

A few minutes ago she had been only too eager to escape Brad's interrogation, but now, reminded afresh of what lay ahead, she got to her feet all of a tremble, her stomach churning.

At the door he draped her fur jacket around her shoulders and, with a proprietary gesture, took her hand and tucked it through his arm.

The evening had remained fine and mild. Above their heads a clear indigo sky was spangled with stars, and a full moon floated like a pale silver balloon.

Once they were moving, the adrenalin pumping into her bloodstream made her walk at a faster pace than normal.

Though he was appreciably taller than she was, he adjusted his stride to suit hers, and they moved easily together, only the occasional brush of thigh against thigh making her falter and the breath catch in her throat.

After a little while he remarked slyly, 'You seem to be in a hurry to get back.'

As she made a determined effort to slow her pace he went on, 'It's a good thing our friend isn't still trying to follow us.'

It took her a moment to catch on. 'You mean the tourist who—?'

'I very much doubt if he was a tourist. I think he'd been paid to watch us. Which means the opposition knows we're here.'

'Oh.'

'Don't look so concerned. It was bound to happen sooner or later.'

His arm tightened, giving her hand a little squeeze. 'And

with much more exciting things to look forward to, who can worry about business problems?

'Unfortunately I only managed a few words with Paul earlier, so before I can forget work and concentrate solely on pleasure, I shall need to contact him again…

'However, I'll try not to keep you waiting too long,' he promised softly, 'and once I've joined you, we'll have the whole night before us to experiment, to find out what gives you the most pleasure…'

The last thing she wanted to do was *enjoy* what was about to happen to her, she thought frantically. But in spite of her normal frigidity, she might be in danger of doing just that.

No, she couldn't let herself enjoy it! The only way she could keep any vestige of pride or self-respect was to remain unmoved, to *suffer* it.

'I don't want to *experiment*…' she began hoarsely. Then, covered in confusion, tried again. 'In the circumstances I'm not concerned about…'

'Your own pleasure?' he suggested as the sentence tailed off. 'Oh, but I am. I've never cared for the ''wham bam, thank you, ma'am'' approach. My own satisfaction is geared to how much my partner is enjoying what's happening…

'No, I suggest we take it nice and slow and easy, that way we'll both gain.' A shade sardonically, he added, 'And once you're into your stride you can show me just how much experience you have got…'

Her throat and mouth dry, chills running up and down her spine, Joanne wondered frantically if it would be best to stay silent or to fight back?

Common sense answered that he was deliberately baiting her, and rising to the bait would just be playing into his hands.

But it might help if she could steer the conversation away

from the coming night. At least it would give her some temporary relief from his tormenting.

Taking a desperate grip on what little remained of her composure, she began as evenly as possible, 'With regard to your business problems, at present I know so little…'

Sighing, he gave her a mocking sidelong glance. 'It's a shameful waste of a lovely night to talk business.'

Focusing straight ahead, she stated firmly, 'If I'm to act as your secretary it would be as well if you put me in the picture.'

Suddenly serious, he agreed, 'You may be right…

'Well, in a nutshell, the problems the Dragon Line have been experiencing were at first thought to be the ordinary, everyday problems that trouble any business. But gradually it became clear there was more to it than that…'

'A form of industrial sabotage?'

'Yes, though on a fairly small scale. That's when I sent Paul over to try and sort things out.

'He laid a trap and caught the person responsible, a cargo-handler named Mussen. The man was aggrieved because his brother, who he firmly believed to be innocent, had been discharged from the DL hotel staff for petty pilfering.

'On my instructions, after a good talking-to, Mussen was allowed to keep his job, which, with an ailing wife and four young children, he badly needed.

'His brother was also reinstated at a somewhat lower level with a promise that, after a six-month probationary period, he should have his old post, as chief desk clerk, back.

'That should have put an end to the problems, and for a while it seemed to have done. Then more worrying things began to happen…'

Only half listening, unable to wean her thoughts away from what the coming night might bring, Joanne asked abstractedly, 'What kind of things?'

'Mostly mechanical failures. For instance, the *Midnight Dragon* car ferry was unable to sail because the main doors couldn't be made watertight.

'Then a steam valve stuck, causing an explosion in one of the boiler rooms—though without any serious casualties, thank the lord…

'Because this time the sabotage could have had very serious consequences, we considered calling in the police. But both Mussen and his brother had alibis, and after digging around for a while Paul couldn't find any real evidence to prove that the boiler-room incident had been anything but accidental.

'After some thought we decided to hang on, and keep everything under wraps. The DSL has an excellent safety record, and if that sort of thing got out it would only destroy confidence and do a great deal of harm to the line's reputation.'

'But that wasn't the end of the problems?'

'No. Things were quiet for a while, and we both hoped that the situation was back to normal. But we were wrong. Over the last couple of weeks it's all started up again.

'A ship's security officer who disturbed an intruder was attacked and left suffering from mild concussion… And in the early hours of yesterday morning a fire broke out in a storeroom of one of our hotels.

'Thanks to an alert and well-trained night security guard, it was dealt with quickly. The damage was kept to a minimum, and, even more importantly, none of the guests were disturbed.

'Only the guard and the manager know about it and they'll keep it to themselves…'

By now they had reached the area of crooked streets and picturesque architecture that Joanne recognised as being not far from the hotel. In a few minutes they would be back. The thought made her palms grow clammy and turned her knees to water.

Making an effort to keep her mind on what he was telling her, she asked, 'You don't think the fire could have been accidental?'

'The guard, who is an ex-fireman, was quite satisfied that it had been started deliberately…'

At that moment they reached the hotel and, pausing on the pavement, Joanne tilted back her head to gaze up at the family of dragons silhouetted against the night sky.

'Would you like to meet the rest?' Brad asked.

'The rest?'

'The rest of the Lofoten dragons.'

He ushered her round the side of the building and through a high wooden gate into a leafy, lantern-lit garden.

An enchanted garden, Joanne found herself thinking as she gazed around her.

The moonlight bleached the scene, turning trees and plants alike to a weird, unearthly silver. Only within the pools of light cast by the lanterns did the autumn colours come to glowing life.

A flight of shallow steps led down from the paved terrace to several different levels. On one side, and seeming to spring from nowhere, a shallow stream chuckled along a fern-hung gully, while paths wound between rocky outcrops, and climbed to secret places.

Brad took her hand, his touch sending a quiver through her, and led her down a moonlit path until they came to a humpbacked bridge that spanned the stream.

On the far side was a wooden summer house, the lantern-lit porch furnished with a couple of reclining chairs.

Having settled her into one, he dropped down beside her and, waving a hand at the rising ground opposite, said, 'There! What do you think?'

They blended in so well that even in the bright moonlight it took her a little while to spot them, and when she finally did surprise made her laugh aloud.

The rocky hillside was swarming with dragons of all

shapes and sizes. A whole family of them, from monsters to babies. Some obviously playing; others sleeping; one peering at them from the undergrowth; another scratching itself.

All different characters. All friendly.

'Aren't they marvellous!' she exclaimed.

'I used to love them as a boy, then when I got to be a teenager and put away childish things, I decided they were a bit twee...'

'And now?'

'Now I think they suit the place.'

'How do they come to be here?'

'The ones on the roof date from when the house was built, but the rest were commissioned when the garden was landscaped some seventy years ago.

'My grandfather, who was the youngest child in the family, and the only boy, loved dragons. They were put here to please him; which they did for the rest of his days.'

It was a nice story, and told in a wonderfully romantic spot. There had been an absence of romance in her life, Joanne thought, and unconsciously sighed for what she had missed.

As though answering that sigh, Brad commented, 'It's a beautiful night.'

'Yes,' she agreed.

With a teasing glance, he added, 'Ideal for lovers, wouldn't you agree?'

Reaching across, he took her hand and, raising it to his lips, dropped a kiss into the palm.

The romantic little gesture made her tremble and set her yearning. Scared stiff by her own treacherous reactions, she snatched her hand away and said jerkily, 'No, I wouldn't.'

Catching hold of her jacket, which she was still wearing loose around her shoulders, she jumped to her feet.

He rose too, seeming to tower over her. 'So what would

you consider ideal? A change of scene? A new moon to wish on? A different companion?'

'The latter.'

'Well, at least you're being honest. Which is a change from last night. Then you said, and I quote: ''I've always found handsome, powerful men like you a real turn-on.'''

Cupping her chin, he tilted her face and studied it in the lantern-light, before saying with evident satisfaction, 'Yes, I should just think so!'

His words made her fiery blush deepen even more.

He laughed softly and, his voice considering, asked, 'So, if you don't want to enjoy a little kiss what shall we talk about?'

'I really don't know,' she muttered.

'Last night you knew. If I remember rightly, you said, ''I'd much rather talk about *you*, Mr Lancing''.'

He gave such a good impression of the 'girly' voice she had used that if she hadn't been so wound-up she would have laughed.

Damn him! she thought vexedly. Oh, damn him!

When she remained silent he sighed theatrically. 'Well, if we can't find anything to talk about I'll just *have* to kiss you.'

Releasing her chin, he drew the edges of her jacket together over her breasts, trapping her arms inside, while he stood gazing down at her thoughtfully.

Her dark eyes looked wide and frightened, and the soft fur gave her face a lovely, luminous quality that he found quite enchanting.

As she stared up at him he asked with smooth mockery, 'All braced for the ordeal?'

A surge of nervous excitement dried her mouth and made butterflies dance in her stomach as, holding her breath, she waited with a kind of helpless hunger, horrified to realise that she *wanted* him to kiss her.

Experienced as he was, he must have known, but even so he took his time about it.

When he finally bent his dark head, and touched his lips to the corner of her mouth, she froze into complete immobility.

After a moment his lips began to travel lightly over hers, bestowing a series of soft plucking kisses that tantalised and tormented without satisfying her hunger for him. When they moved away to graze over her jaw and the soft skin beneath her chin, trembling, eyes closed, lips a little parted, she waited in an agony of suspense.

Then, so unexpectedly that she staggered, she found she was free.

'There, now, the ordeal's over,' he told her cheerfully. 'That wasn't so bad, was it?'

Instead of relief, she felt a blinding anger.

He'd done it purposely of course. Setting her up. Making her wait. Deliberately teasing her.

'Dear me,' he murmured, 'you look quite disappointed. Did you want me to kiss you properly? Or would *you* like to kiss *me*?'

'I'd sooner cut my throat.'

Swinging on her heel, she set off back across the bridge and up the path towards the house.

He caught her up and, walking by her side, kept pace effortlessly. Though she refused to look at him, she felt convinced that he was smiling.

When they reached the terrace he said, 'We can go in this way,' and, opening one of a pair of doors that weren't unlike French windows, ushered her into what appeared to be a breakfast-room.

'Would you like a nightcap of any kind before we go upstairs?'

'No, thank you.'

The minute the words were out, she wished she had said yes. It would have given her a little more breathing-space.

'Then we can go this way.'

He escorted her through to an inner hall, up a back stair-case, and along a short stretch of corridor to their suite. Having let them into the living-room, he switched on the light and dropped the latch behind them, making her feel trapped.

As she hovered uncertainly he slipped her jacket from her shoulders and, moving aside her curtain of dark, silky hair, touched his lips to the warmth of her nape.

Shuddering, she turned at bay.

Looking anything but concerned, he suggested, 'If you'd like to go ahead and get ready for bed, I'll join you as soon as I've had a word with Paul.'

Her stomach tied itself in knots.

She'd die if he touched her.

She'd die if he didn't.

'Please don't hurry on my account,' she said fervently.

He laughed. Despite the fact that she was easy to scare, she didn't lack either courage or spirit.

'In fact, if you *never* come it will be too soon—'

The words ended in a little gasp as he took her face between his palms and, running his fingers into her hair, quoted, '"Methinks the lady doth protest too much."' Then sardonically, 'Can it be that you really fancy me?'

Frightened to death in case he had guessed the conflict-ing emotions that filled her, she muttered, 'I *loathe* you.'

A glint in his eye, he said, 'Now you've hurt my feel-ings... And just when I thought we were getting on well.'

Bending his head until his lips were only inches from hers, he suggested, 'I think I should have a kiss to make up for it.'

'I don't want you to kiss me,' she said thickly.

'Would it help if you pretended I was Trevor?'

'No, it wouldn't.'

'Thank the lord for that,' he said piously, and before she could catch her breath his mouth was covering hers.

If she had expected the same kind of punitive kiss she'd been subjected to the previous night, she couldn't have been more wrong.

Gentle, rather than forceful, his mouth coaxed and beguiled, his tongue-tip tracing the outline of her lips before slipping between them to tease the sensitive inner skin.

When, unable to hold out against him, her lips parted, he deepened the kiss.

Like a lighted match being dropped into a pool of petrol, fire exploded inside her, and for perhaps the first time in her life she knew what it was like to be consumed by passion. A white-hot passion that seared her very soul and melted every bone in her body.

As he felt her grow limp his arms went around her and his kisses became ardent and demanding, asking for, and getting, a response that only served to add to the conflagration.

When he finally lifted his head, unable to stand, she clung to him, dazed and devastated, only gradually becoming aware that somewhere close at hand a phone was ringing.

Though he was breathing as if he had just run a race, his recovery was light years ahead of her own. Steering her to the nearest chair, he pushed her into it, and went into his office.

She was vaguely aware that he was speaking, without making any sense of the words.

After a moment or two he returned to say, 'That was Paul. I need to talk to him, so if you'd like to go to bed…?'

She looked up at him, a hectic flush on her cheeks, her eyes wide and unfocused, and got unsteadily to her feet.

'I'd better give you a hand.' Stooping, he picked her up and carried her through to the bedroom, setting her down carefully.

Having switched on the bedside lamp, he drew the

greeny-blue folk-weave curtains and asked, 'Do you need any help to get undressed?'

Made speechless by the effortless way he'd carried her, she shook her head.

'Then I'll join you as soon as I've finished talking to Paul.'

The door closed quietly behind him.

CHAPTER SIX

SHAKEN to the core, Joanne found it was several minutes before she could pull herself together enough to go through to the bathroom and prepare for bed.

As she creamed off her make-up she looked at the woman in the mirror. Though the dark hair and eyes, the shape of the face and the features were the same, it was a stranger who stared back at her.

In place of the usual pale composure there was a pink flush lying along the high cheekbones, and the blue eyes were so dark they looked almost black.

The mouth too was different. Instead of the starved, pinched look she had started to glimpse at times, it had the soft ripeness of a mouth that had just been thoroughly kissed.

She had got used to thinking of herself as a woman who lacked something, who was next-door to frigid. A woman to whom sexual love and passion would always be a stranger. Someone *incomplete*.

Now her whole conception of herself had been changed, and for good.

If the man who had worked this miracle had been anyone other than who he was she would have gone down on her knees and given thanks.

Perhaps she still should, she thought, there was a lot to be thankful for. For the first time in her life she felt emotionally whole. Complete.

Though Brad Lancing was lecherous and rotten to the core, there was something inside her that responded to his maleness, that sang into life when he touched her.

If only she could feel that kind of passion for a decent

man; a man she could love and marry, who would make a good father; a man she could spend the rest of her life with.

Catching sight of the ring on her finger, she thought of Trevor, and knew without a doubt that he wasn't that man.

The kind of blazing response she had given Brad would frighten poor Trevor half to death. He wasn't emotionally equipped to handle it.

Nor inspire it, for that matter.

He was the sort of man who felt more at home with a nice, steady, low-key existence. Narrow and grey.

Seeing things clearly now, she guessed that the main reason, maybe the *only* reason, he had asked her to marry him was that he believed she was safe and undemanding. That she wouldn't rock the boat by asking for more than he could give.

The same reasons that had made her consider accepting him.

She sighed, it just showed how emotionally unawakened, how blind, she must have been to even *think* of accepting a man who was willing to marry only because his mother wanted grandchildren.

Sighing, she admitted what she had always known. Trevor was still tied to his mother's apron strings, and even if he married he would allow his mother to keep on running his life…

No, now she knew what it was like to feel whole, she couldn't marry Trevor, and she could only be thankful that, rather than accepting his proposal, she had asked for time to think. It would make it somewhat easier to give him back his ring.

If only she hadn't agreed to wear it in the first place…

The fact that she *had* would no doubt add to his anger and disappointment, but it was much too late for regrets, and common sense told her that he himself wouldn't be seriously hurt, only his pride.

Though what if, by turning Trevor down, she lost out

completely? As Milly was fond of pointing out, she was no Miss World. What if no other man ever wanted her, except perhaps for a brief fling?

Even now, with her new-found confidence in herself, she knew she wasn't the type to go in for affairs.

But if she was going to live at all she wanted some colour and excitement and love in her life, so she would take the chance.

When she had brushed out her hair she started, naked, for the bedroom. Her hand was on the doorknob, when she froze.

She had been so taken up with Brad's effect on her that she hadn't given any thought to the man himself. Suppose he was already lying there in bed, waiting for her?

Her throat closing up with a mixture of nervousness, anticipation and embarrassment, she stood rooted to the spot, listening to her own breathing and heartbeat.

Now she knew what a devastating effect his kisses had on her, she doubted her ability to stay unmoved. And after her helpless response he must feel very confident that, sexually at least, she would make the kind of companion he wanted.

But after teasing her about her 'experience' it might come as a shock when he discovered, as he was bound to, how utterly *inexperienced* she was.

After a minute or so, knowing it was necessary to get a grip, she read herself the Riot Act. There was no way she could stay lurking in the bathroom indefinitely. If Brad decided to come looking for her it would make her feel both stupid and cowardly.

The least she could do was go out there and face him with her head held high. Pulling on a towelling robe, she tied the belt and, filled with a kind of panicky excitement, threw open the door.

The bed was empty, and so was the room.

She hardly knew whether to be relieved or sorry. In some

ways the *waiting* was the worst. It would surely be less
traumatic to get it over with.

Having hung the robe back behind the bathroom door,
she took Trevor's ring from her finger and dropped it into
one of the case's zipped inner pockets, before finding a
nightdress and pulling it on.

A mid-calf-length shift made of ivory satin, it had shoestring shoulder straps and was split down to the waist, the
two halves of material held together by a series of matching
bows.

Complete with a second, coffee-coloured nightie, and a
matching negligee, it had been a so-far unworn Christmas
gift from Milly and Duncan.

'I thought it was time you had something young and
glamorous,' Milly had said bluntly, 'instead of those dreadful little orphan Annie things you wear.'

But Joanne had been happy with her Victorian cotton
nighties, until Brad had appeared so obviously amused.

When she had been packing, remembering that amusement, a kind of perverse pride had made her take the satin
rather than the cotton.

Now she was glad she had.

Putting the negligee on the bottom of the bed, she
climbed in and, pulling up the duvet, hesitated. Should she
sit up with the light on?

But if she did she would appear to be waiting for him.

Perhaps it was better to switch it off and look settled?

Deciding on the latter, she turned off the lamp and snuggled down, closing her eyes. Surely he would hurry through
his business? Though she was anything but experienced,
she hadn't the slightest doubt that he had been as aroused
as she was.

Her whole body newly awakened and eager, totally unable to relax, the waiting seemed endless.

She found herself thinking ahead. How it would be when

he came to her... When he kissed her and touched her...
When he made love to her...

In the darkness her cheeks grew hot.

Only it wouldn't *be* love, she reminded herself. It would
be lust... That sobering thought should have depressed her,
but somehow it failed to. Knowing only too well what kind
of man he was, she still wanted him with a hunger that
amazed her.

Though the common-sense part of her knew that she
would bitterly regret it later, pride seemed a cold companion compared to the urgency of her need.

In the past, when Milly had got involved with unsuitable
boys, Joanne had wondered vexedly why the girl hadn't
exercised more self-control.

Now she knew.

Impatiently, she switched on the light and looked at her
watch. More than an hour had gone by. What on earth
could be keeping him?

Pushing back the duvet, she got out of bed and opened
the door into the living-room. The curtains were drawn
across the windows and the room was in semi-darkness,
apart from the red-gold glow thrown out by the stove.

He must be working at his desk.

But the door to his office appeared to be slightly ajar,
and she could see no lights burning there either.

Curiosity made her pad across to push the door wider
and peer inside. Brad wasn't at his desk and the room was
empty. He must have gone out.

Disappointment bitter on her tongue, she turned.

He had made the couch up as a bed and was lying on
his back, the covers pulled up to his hips, his hands clasped
behind his head. Beneath the dark brows his eyes gleamed
in the firelight.

Above the waist he was wearing nothing, and the same
below, she guessed. He looked like an advert for some
sexy, masculine body-splash.

Totally disconcerted, she just stood and stared at him.

'Well, well, well…' he murmured. 'I thought you would be asleep by now.'

Somehow she found herself saying, 'I couldn't sleep.'

'Frustration is hell,' he agreed, his voice wry. 'But, as you've come to me, I guess we can do something about it.' He held out his hand.

Shamefaced and desperately self-conscious, she stood rooted to the spot, making no attempt to take the proffered hand.

'Come here,' he ordered softly.

Still she made no move.

'If I have to come and get you…'

He left the threat unfinished, but it was enough to get her unsteady legs working, and as though mesmerised she took a few steps towards the couch.

'Closer,' he said inexorably.

When she was standing beside him he reached out and lightly stroked the smooth ivory satin covering her upper thigh, making every nerve in her body leap in response.

'Though I thought the Victorian look had a certain charm, I must say I prefer this. It's a wonderful combination of virginal and sexy.'

Her mouth desert-dry, she waited.

He picked up her left hand. 'I see you've taken off Trevor's ring.'

Thinking ruefully that he didn't miss a thing, she said, 'I decided it was a mistake to wear it.'

'Why was it a mistake?'

'Well, I…I realised I didn't care for him enough.'

'You told me you loved him.'

'Perhaps love was too strong a word. I'm…fond of him.'

'But he loves you?'

'I don't think so.'

'When I asked if you'd received a declaration of undying love, you said yes.'

'It wasn't true,' she admitted. 'Love was never mentioned. He regards me as *suitable*.'

'So the engagement's off?'

'It was never really on,' she admitted.

'Then your sister's version was the right one?' he remarked with satisfaction.

Joanne nodded mutely.

'Good.' Surprising her, he added, 'I wasn't altogether comfortable with the idea of making off with another man's fiancée…

'Tell me, why did you wear the ring?'

'Trevor had put it on my finger, and to please him I agreed to keep it on while I made up my mind. Now I have.'

'And this is your final decision?'

'Yes. In the circumstances I've decided I can't marry him.'

'In the circumstances…' Brad repeated softly. 'If it wasn't for the *circumstances*, would you have married him?'

She answered truthfully, 'I might have done.'

Watching his brows knit together in a frown, she added, 'But I realise now that it would have been a sad mistake.'

'I must say, I'm pleased. A marriage like that would never have worked.'

Curiously, she asked, 'What makes you think so?'

'For one thing, you're much too warm and passionate for a cold fish like Trevor…'

It gave her the strangest feeling to hear herself referred to as *passionate*…

'And for another, marriage should involve a twosome, rather than a threesome.

'I'm only amazed that you ever considered accepting him in the first place.'

So was she now.

Weakly, she said, 'We had a lot in common…or at least I thought we had…'

Surprising her, Brad remarked, 'I imagine we two have a great deal more. To start with, let's see how sexually compatible we are…'

Tense and waiting, she started to tremble.

He gave the hand he was still holding a sudden jerk, so that with a startled squeak she fell half on top of him.

Throwing an arm around her, he held her to his bare chest and, growling, buried his face against her throat.

That kind of playful rough and tumble was the last thing she had expected and, her dignity momentarily outraged, she put her hands flat-palmed against his chest and tried to 'ever herself away.

Laughing, he rolled, pinning her beneath him so that she was squashed and breathless. Then, finding the tender spot where neck and shoulder meet, he gave her a love bite.

His mouth, and the warmth of his naked body through the thin satin sending shudders of desire running through her, she made a half-strangled protest.

'Don't you like to play?' he asked seriously.

'It's just that you took me by surprise…'

'I intended to. It releases the tension.' He kissed the tip of her nose. 'Didn't Trevor ever play love games?'

'No.'

'What about your other lovers?'

Uncertain how to answer, she stayed silent.

Lifting a dark brow, he hazarded, 'Or maybe there haven't been any other lovers?'

When she still said nothing he added, 'Never mind, in a little while I'll find out to my own satisfaction…and yours too, I hope. But first I want to look at you…'

His weight lifted, and a moment later, finding his feet, he had scooped her off the couch and laid her down on the thick goatskin rug that lay in front of the stove.

His face intent, absorbed, he untied the bows holding the

bodice of her nightdress together and, slipping the straps from her shoulders, eased it past her waist and over her hips.

As he stared down at her body lit by the firelight's glow he caught his breath. Long-legged and slender, her skin flawless, her breasts small and firm and beautifully shaped above a narrow waist and flaring hips, she was the loveliest thing he'd ever seen.

'You look as perfect as a golden statue,' he said softly.

'I'm anything but perfect,' she objected breathlessly. 'I have a mole.'

'So you have.' He sounded fascinated. 'Which makes you even more perfect. I've never really fancied making love to a statue.'

Bending his head, he kissed the small dark mole that lay like a beauty spot on her flat stomach, before nuzzling his face against the softness of her breasts.

The slight roughness of his skin added an extra dimension to the pleasure, and she gasped.

Lifting his head a little, he said, 'Bristles can be ruinous to a delicate skin. If I'd realised I would have shaved again. I still can if you—'

'No! No, you don't need to…' She couldn't bear it if he left her now. As he hesitated, as if not totally convinced, she added fervently, 'I *like* it, really I do,' and heard his quiet chuckle.

Then, closing his eyes, as though to add to the tactile pleasure, he let his lips rove over her breast, searching blindly for a nipple.

When, finding one, he took it into his mouth and suckled sweetly, she began to make soft little mewing sounds in her throat, and when his hand slid downwards to explore and add to her pleasure she found herself imploring, 'Please… Oh, please…'

But, refusing to hurry, he led her through a maze of sensual delight, taking time to touch and taste every inch of her, leaving her whole body alive and quivering with sensation.

When she thought she could stand no more of such exquisite torment and begged him hoarsely to stop he laughed softly, and said, 'My little innocent, I've only just started.'

By the time she felt the weight of his body, into sensual overload, she was convinced she could experience nothing further. But once again he proved her wrong by entering her and lifting her to heights of ecstasy she'd never even dreamt of.

Afterwards, lying with her head pillowed on his shoulder, his body half supporting hers, the glow from the stove warming her bare flesh, she knew herself to be completely and utterly happy.

His cheek resting on her hair, he asked gently, 'Why did you tell me you'd had lots of experience?'

'I'm not sure,' she admitted. 'It just seemed to be part of the game we were playing.'

'A game you had no stomach for, judging by the look on your face. Tell me, Joanne, how many lovers have you had?'

'None apart from you,' she admitted.

'That's what I thought, but I could hardly believe it. Did something happen to put you off sex?'

'No. It was just that nothing *good* happened. I didn't seem able to respond... I began to think I *couldn't*...but still part of me wanted a home of my own and children...'

'So that's why you considered marrying a man like Trevor?'

'Yes.'

He shook his head. 'Such a colourless existence might well have destroyed a woman like you... Or at least done you as much harm as I have.'

'You haven't done me any harm,' she denied, yawning.

'Through forcing you to come to Norway with me, I've altered the course of your life.'

Heavy lids drooping, drifting on a warm sea of contentment, she said thickly, 'I can only be grateful for that.'

She was deeply asleep when he finally eased himself
free, and, having collected her nightdress, stooped to gather
up her slight weight, murmuring, 'Better take you back to
bed. It'll soon start to get cool.'

When he had carried her though to the bedroom he
tucked her in, dropped her nightie over a chair, and bent to
kiss her softly before switching off the lamp.

Bright sunshine was slanting in through a chink in the curtains when Joanne drifted slowly and languorously to the
surface, aware that she was in bed, but with no recollection
of how she had got there.

Her last memory was of lying in Brad's arms in front of
the glowing stove. The euphoria she had felt then was still
with her.

Encased in a golden bubble of happiness, she sighed and
stretched luxuriously. Her body felt tender in places, but as
sleek and satisfied as a cat sated on cream. Her mind, still
in a blissful dreamlike trance, was as yet undisturbed by
the realities of the situation.

For a moment or two she lay savouring this wonderful
and extraordinary feeling of joy, then, needing to see the
man who had given her such a priceless gift, she turned her
head.

The pillow beside her was smooth and undisturbed. For
whatever reason, Brad had returned to the couch rather than
share the bed.

Frowning, she wondered why. Surely it couldn't be on
ethical grounds?

Or could it?

In some ways he was turning out to be not at all the kind
of man she had first thought him.

Though he had ruthlessly coerced her into coming to
Norway with him, he had admitted that he wasn't altogether

comfortable with the idea of 'making off' with another man's fiancée…

Still, she had explained that there was not, and never had been, a real engagement, so what was the problem?

At least she and Brad were grown adults and free, and if it was the circumstances that were troubling him, as he had pointed out, *she* had gone to *him*, so he couldn't be accused of forcing her in any way…

She had gone to him… The remembrance of that should have made her cringe, should have made her feel ashamed and humiliated.

But somehow it didn't.

For once in her life she had acted completely out of character, brushing aside both common sense and propriety.

She should be eaten up with remorse, but even the sight of her nightdress hanging over a chair couldn't make her feel sorry. Couldn't make her regret what had happened.

And surely Brad wouldn't?

Though he must have known how totally naïve she was in sexual matters, he had clearly enjoyed making love to her. So why had he returned to sleep alone on the couch? Why hadn't he got into bed beside her?

If he *had* she could have snuggled up against him, let her bare leg brush his… This time *she* could have touched *him*, let her fingers find the small leathery nipples, and the ripple of muscles beneath the smooth skin, run her hand down his flat belly to play with the dark, silky curls of pubic hair…

Shocked by her own unbridled sensuality, she jumped out of bed and hurried naked into the bathroom to clean her teeth and shower.

As she stood beneath the jet of hot water, soaping her breasts and recalling how Brad's hands had caressed and fondled them, all at once she thought of Milly, and felt absurdly guilty.

But why should she feel guilty?

It wasn't as if she had set out to steal the man her sister fancied. Her only concern had been to save Milly's marriage, and hopefully she had done just that.

Now the young pair had started a new life in Scotland, with a bit of luck Milly would soon have forgotten the foolish crush she had had on her boss.

Though it was ironic in the extreme that, having saved Milly from such a dangerous and potentially destructive relationship, she had been unable to save herself.

And now she wouldn't even if she could.

When Joanne had dressed in an oatmeal linen skirt and top, she brushed out her black hair and, after the briefest hesitation, left it loose around her shoulders.

As her lover liked it…

The thought sprang into her mind, sending a fizz of excitement through her. She had never imagined herself having a lover. And certainly not a wonderful sensual man like Brad.

Heading for the living-room, her heart beating faster, she wondered what he would do, how he would treat her. Would he hold out his hand and smile? Or would he take her in his arms and kiss her?

In the event he did neither.

When she opened the door and walked into a room full of fresh air and sunlight, he tossed aside the paper he was reading, and rose to his feet, gravely courteous.

Dressed in stone-coloured trousers and a black polo-necked sweater, he looked so virile and attractive that he took her breath away.

Though she hadn't been able to wait to see him, the moment their eyes met she found herself blushing painfully.

'Good morning. I hope you slept well?'

While pleasant and friendly, neither his tone nor his attitude were remotely lover-like.

'Y-yes, thank you.' Disconcerted, she found herself stammering slightly.

'I was about to give you a call. Breakfast should be here any minute.'

Right on cue, there was a tap at the door.

'Come in,' he invited.

The door opened to admit a young, fair-haired girl wheeling a breakfast trolley.

'Thank you, Lys. You can leave it there. I'll see to it.'

She gave him a quick, eager smile and left without a word, closing the door quietly behind her.

Pushing back the couch, from which the bedding had been removed, Brad pulled the trolley in front of the open window and placed a chair at either end.

Then, turning to Joanne, who was hovering uncertainly, he asked, 'Where would you like to sit?'

'I don't mind in the slightest,' she answered, and took the chair he pulled out for her.

He sat down opposite and raised an enquiring brow. 'Tea or coffee?'

'Coffee, please.'

In spite of—or maybe *because* of—the previous night's intimacy, they were acting like two strangers, she thought in dismay as he lifted the coffee-pot and filled both their cups.

'Now, what would you like to eat?'

The trolley was set with crusty bread, jam, cold meat, various cheeses, and fish.

She was about to plump for bread and jam when, a gleam in his eye, he suggested, 'If you feel brave enough, why don't you sample the herring?'

Her heart lifting in response to that hint of devilment, she agreed, 'I'd love to.'

He helped her to a generous portion, and passed her the plate.

Accepting it with a word of thanks, she added quizzically, 'I strongly suspect you were hoping to call me a coward?'

He smiled at her, and her heart turned right over. 'A coward is the last thing I'd call you...though I admit to being surprised. None of the females I've known would touch it. Though it's extremely tasty.'

Watching him help himself to some, she said, 'As a matter of fact you're preaching to the converted. I adore kippers.'

He threw back his head and laughed. 'I'm beginning to realise you're a woman of many parts.'

Very conscious of him, of his powerful masculinity, she tried hard to concentrate on her meal, but each time her eyes inadvertently strayed in his direction she found he was watching her.

Growing uncomfortable beneath that steady scrutiny, and needing something to say, she asked, 'Did you get in touch with Paul Randall?'

'Yes.' Brad frowned.

'Something wrong?'

'There was another spot of trouble during the evening. Nothing major, but enough to slightly injure a crew member, and prevent one of the ships from sailing.

'The problem is, the longer this sabotage goes on, the more chance there is of someone getting seriously hurt.'

'And you really don't think that whoever's behind it will stop?'

Brad shook his head. 'Mr X, if I may so call him, has been stepping up the attacks. I strongly suspect with the intention of bringing me over here.'

'Why should he want to do that?'

'It's always easier to deal with the opposition on home ground. But I may yet surprise him by winning.'

'I don't see how you can hope to win when you don't know where the next attack's going to be.'

'Certainly an open, all-out war would be a lot easier to fight.'

Wryly, he added, 'That's no doubt why this person prefers an undercover campaign. As you remarked when we were leaving the airport, it's all very cloak-and-daggerish…'

Seeing her faint shiver, he said reassuringly, 'There's no need to worry. I can't imagine you'd be in the slightest danger.'

'Which means *you* might?'

'Though it may sound melodramatic, there is a possibility. Paul has already had a bit of bother which might, or might not, have been an accident.'

'What kind of bother?'

'The brakes on his car failed. Luckily he was back home and just coasting into the garage, so the only damage was a cracked headlight.

'I've suggested he keeps quiet about it, and gets the car properly examined to see if the brakes have been tampered with.'

Getting to his feet, he stretched, lithe as a big cat. 'But that's enough of problems… As it's Sunday, I thought rather than work I'd play hookey.'

Wondering if that meant he was going to leave her to her own devices, she said, 'Oh.'

'What's the matter? Did you want to work?'

She shook her head.

'Then as it's such a lovely day, I'll take you up Mount Floyen. At the top there's a look-out point that gives you a bird's-eye view of the town.'

His manner was that of a pleasant, slightly detached host, but still she felt her spirits soaring. He wasn't intending to walk away and leave her. They would be together.

And, strangely enough, being with him was the only thing that really mattered.

'There's no rain forecast,' he went on, 'so you shouldn't need more than a jacket with you, just in case it turns cool.'

'I'll get one,' she said eagerly.

Each wearing a light jacket, they walked for perhaps half

a mile through the sunny and pleasant streets of Bergen, until they came to what appeared to be the glass entrance to a station.

'Floyen is over a thousand feet above sea-level,' Brad told her, 'so most people take the *Floybanen*.'

The cable car was busy with rucksack-laden tourists, but they got a seat without too much difficulty.

Disturbed by the pressure of his muscular thigh against her own, Joanne stared determinedly through the window as they climbed steadily.

There were several intermediate stops on the way to the top but, totally distracted, her mind on other, more personal, things, she took in very little.

At the top Brad helped her off, and, taking her hand, led her out onto an airy platform apparently suspended in space.

She gasped at the view. Spread far below them, glowing with autumn colours, Bergen looked like a perfect scale model, its necklace of green and gold islands set like gems in a sea of lapis lazuli.

'Isn't it magnificent?' she breathed.

He smiled. 'I've always thought so.'

Having stood for quite a time admiring the view, they strolled the length of the platform and turned towards a small village.

As they reached a wooden bench Brad instructed, 'Wait here a minute.'

Obediently Joanne sat down and watched his broad shoulders disappear into a shop.

When he returned he was carrying two long, curly cones. Handing her one, he said with a grin, 'I couldn't let you miss out on one of my favourite boyhood treats.'

Sitting side by side in the sun, they started on the delectable concoction of ice cream mingled with candied oranges, apricots, cherries and nuts.

Nibbling around the top of her crisp cone, as she had

often done as a child, she thought about the man by her side.

Brad had called her a woman of many parts. Now she was beginning to realise that the same could be said for him. The worldly, sophisticated man she knew had vanished, to be replaced by someone carefree and boyish.

Someone she could love.

CHAPTER SEVEN

No! REMEMBERING his playboy reputation, remembering Milly, how could she possibly think that?

She could *never* love Brad.

Sexual attraction was one thing. Physical. Fleeting. A surface magnetism that would eventually wither and die for lack of roots. No emotions needed to be involved. Except the obvious.

Real love was something totally different. Deep and lasting, a seed that, having once taken root, grew and flourished and transformed completely. An emotion that, if one was lucky, would change and endure, and last a lifetime.

Though how would she know that? She who had never been in love… Yet she *did* know, and what she felt for Brad was merely sexual attraction, she told herself firmly.

All the same, he was completely irresistible.

Glancing surreptitiously at him, she saw that his eyes were narrowed against the sun, the thick, sooty lashes almost brushing his hard cheeks; his dark hair was slightly ruffled, and there was a fragment of apricot on his lower lip.

While she watched him, fascinated, he gathered it up neatly with the tip of his tongue, and then, as if sensing her regard, turned his head to glance at her. Though she felt the colour rise in her cheeks, she was unable to look away, caught and held by those eyes. Fascinating eyes, the colour of deep mossy pools, with a ring of even darker green surrounding the iris, and tiny flecks of gold swimming in their clear depths.

As she gazed at him, mesmerised, he broke the spell by saying lightly, 'Aren't we a messy pair?' and, leaning forward, licked away a smear of ice cream from the corner of her mouth.

That erotic little action made her heart start to race and her stomach fold in on itself.

Looking hurriedly away, she returned her attention to her ice-cream cone and, finishing it to the last crumb, sucked her sticky fingers like an urchin.

Brad reached for his jacket and, having fished in the pocket, produced a small bottle of water and a packet of tissues. When he'd dampened a wad, he handed her half.

'Thank you. Were you ever a boy scout?'

Grinning, he wiped his own hands and said, 'No. It's experience that's taught me to be prepared.'

Cleaning her fingers, she said contentedly, 'That was absolutely delightful.'

'And so are you.'

She caught her breath audibly, oddly moved by the sweetness of the unexpected compliment, and her hands weren't quite steady when she handed him the tissues to dispose of.

Dropping them into a nearby litter bin, he suggested gravely, 'I thought we might go for a walk now, if that suits you?'

'That suits me fine,' she agreed, and rose without looking at him, afraid he would see the turmoil of emotions that filled her.

'I doubt very much if that weirdo has bothered to follow us up here,' Brad went on, 'but if he has it'll give him some exercise.'

He sounded so laid-back about it that, unwilling to tarnish the brightness of the day, Joanne refused to worry.

Tucking her hand through his arm, he added, 'If we take a circular route we'll be back in this area just in time for a late lunch.'

'Sounds ideal.'

It was a perfect autumn day, still and balmy, the thin

golden air exhilarating as champagne as they took a sun-dappled path through the scented pine woods.

Enjoying the movement and the feel of the springy carpet of brown pine needles beneath their feet, they walked mostly in companionable silence, with only the odd remark being passed.

It was approaching two o'clock when, having almost completed the loop, they reached a fairy-tale hotel perched on a tremendous overhang.

'I thought we'd have lunch at the Trondheim,' Brad said. 'There's a wonderful view from the terrace.'

It was so idyllic that, too happy to speak, she nodded wordlessly.

After freshening up they were shown to a table for two beneath a gaily-striped umbrella. There they were served with a delicately chilled white wine and an excellent salad.

The leisurely meal over, they were just drinking their coffee, when a well-dressed blonde woman of statuesque proportions advanced on their table, crying, 'Brad, darling! Where on earth have you been? I've been trying to get hold of you to invite you to my party, but your office told me you were away... Why didn't you let me know you were coming?'

'Erika...' Tossing his napkin onto the table, he rose to his feet.

She was somewhere in her early twenties, Joanne guessed, and almost as tall as he was. High heels brought her eyes on a level with his. A moment later she had thrown her arms around his neck and was kissing him full on the lips.

For a moment he stood perfectly still, then, unwinding her arms, he stepped back and surveyed her. Silvery hair hung straight and glossy, framing an oval face with perfect features and eyes of a pale, glacial blue.

'Erika, you're looking as beautiful as ever,' he remarked with cool politeness.

Then, turning to his companion, 'Joanne, may I introduce Ms Reiersen? Erika, this is my secretary, Miss Winslow.'

'How do you do?' Joanne murmured.

The blonde's glance slid over her dismissively, and without deigning to reply she said to Brad, 'How long have you been here?'

'We flew in yesterday.'

'I'm seriously angry that you came to Bergen without letting me know. Daddy will be too.'

'It was a spur-of-the-moment decision.'

'Well, I'll forgive you if you come to my party.'

'When is it?'

'Tonight…so, you see, you're just in time… It's to celebrate my divorce. As of now, I'm a free woman.' She displayed her ringless fingers.

'Well, I—'

'I know Daddy will expect you to be there.'

At Brad's slight frown, she added hurriedly, 'Even though it's a party I'm sure he'll want to talk business, but I won't let him monopolise you, I promise…

'Oh, and Paul Randall will be coming, so you really can't let the side down.'

Joanne found the blonde's desperation, and the reason for the party, both sad and pathetic.

A young chap appeared by her side, fair-haired, bearded and brawny, and with a hostile glance at Brad asked, 'Are you about ready, Erika?'

Ignoring him completely, she put a beautifully manicured hand on Brad's arm and urged, 'Promise me you'll be there…'

'I take it the invitation includes Miss Winslow?'

'Why on earth should you want to bring your secretary?' she asked rudely. Then, 'You *will* come?'

His tone regretful, Brad said, 'I'm afraid I've already promised Miss Winslow that I'll take her to the Kirkesen tonight.'

'Well, I'm sure she won't mind—'

'I really don't mind—'

The two women spoke simultaneously.

He shook his head. 'As Miss Winslow is new to Norway, I don't want to leave her sitting in a hotel room on her own.'

'For heaven's sake,' Erika burst out petulantly, 'she's not a child. She can go out on her own if she wants to...'

Apparently seeing by his face that she was wasting her breath, she said ungraciously, 'Oh, very well, bring her if you must. I'll expect you about seven.'

She presented her mouth for his kiss.

He gave her a chaste salute on the cheek.

Obviously disappointed, she turned away.

Her young partner, scowling his displeasure, moved to follow her.

Brad sat down again, remarking, 'Not a very sociable young man at the best of times, and jealousy does nothing to improve his manners...

'And, speaking of manners, I apologise for Erika's rudeness. I hope you don't dislike her for it.'

Sounding tolerant, he added, 'You see, she isn't altogether to blame. She's always been Daddy's little girl and allowed to get away with anything.'

'Of course I don't dislike her. In fact I felt rather sorry for her. It can't be much fun having one's marriage break up.'

'Especially after two other relationships ended in disaster. But that kind of upbringing doesn't encourage the willingness to compromise. Nor does it create a good basis for wedded bliss. And unfortunately she chose to marry her own cousin, which meant they shared a lot of the same faults.'

'How long did the marriage last?'

'They separated after just a few months.'

Just a few months… And now she was celebrating being single again…

As though reading her mind, Brad added, 'To me, divorce smacks of failure. I don't see it as a good reason for having a party. Still, we won't need to stay too long.'

Heartily disliking the whole situation, Joanne said, 'I really think you should go alone.'

'I don't want to go alone. I happen to want you with me.'

'It's very kind of you to be concerned about me, but I really don't mind if you leave me.'

'I've no intention of leaving you.'

She gave up trying to be diplomatic, and said flatly, 'And I've no intention of going to the party when Ms Reiersen so obviously doesn't want me there.'

'Erika may sound a little ungracious, but I'm sure she'll be more than happy to see both of us,' he assured her smoothly.

'Like hell!' Joanne muttered under her breath.

'In any case, *I* want you to go.'

She bit her lip, determined that this time he wouldn't get his way. Wild horses wouldn't drag her to that party.

Watching her mutinous face, he asked, 'Now, would you like some more coffee?'

'No, thank you,' she said distantly.

'Then I think we should be making a move. It's possible to walk down to town via Fjellveien, but I think we've done enough walking today. Especially as we'll no doubt be dancing tonight,' he added deliberately.

When she made no comment, apparently accepting her silence as submission, he tucked her hand through his arm, and they made their way back to the cable car, only to find they had just missed it.

As, forced to wait half an hour for the next one, they sat in silence Joanne found herself wondering about his relationship with Erika. Judging by the way the blonde had kissed him, it must have been a close one.

Had been? Or *still was?* Brad had said something about the young chap being jealous.

But surely any close relationship must have ended, or presumably Brad would have told the blonde he was coming to Bergen…?

It was almost a quarter past six by the time they reached Lofoten. 'I expect you could do with a cup of tea?' Brad suggested.

Having half expected to be hurried straight up to his suite, Joanne relaxed, and asked, 'When did you learn to mind-read?'

A gleam in his eye, he answered succinctly, 'As far as *you're* concerned I find it easy.'

Annoyed with herself for giving him an opening, she wished she had simply said 'Yes, please.'

The lobby was empty, and when Helga looked up to smile and greet them Brad ordered a pot of tea.

Then, having settled Joanne in front of the stove, he said, 'There's something I need to do before we go up, but I'll try not to be long.'

A moment later he had disappeared back through the main entrance, and she caught just a glimpse of him walking quickly past the small-paned windows.

She had finished her second cup of tea and was starting to wonder where on earth he'd got to, when he returned.

'Would you like some tea?' she asked.

He shook his head. 'No time. It's almost seven o'clock now, and you've got some getting-ready to do!'

'If you think for one minute I'm going to that party—' she began fiercely.

'Shhh…' He put a finger to her lips and, glancing in Helga's direction, added quizzically, 'We mustn't fall out in front of the staff… Now, the lift's not here, so the stairs will be quicker.'

The wooden treads creaked comfortably under their weight as, stoking the fires of anger and defiance, she accompanied him up to their suite.

As soon as the door had closed behind them he said, 'Now, we both need to shower and change, and I must order a taxi, so if you want to have a row, make it snappy, because we haven't a lot of time.'

As though to add weight to his words, the grandmother clock chimed the hour.

'I don't want to have a row,' she said as calmly as possible.

'Good. In that case, we can both start getting ready.'

She defied him. 'I've no need to get ready. I really don't want to go to the party.'

He shook his head reprovingly. 'Perhaps you've forgotten, it's what *I* want that counts, and I want you to go with me.'

'I want to stay here.'

'But you don't have a choice,' he said flatly. 'Now, please go and get ready.'

'I won't.'

Though his expression didn't change, she could feel the force of his anger and was suddenly scared stiff of it.

But what could he do to her? He wouldn't hurt her.

Or would he? Even as the thought crossed her mind she knew with certainty that, no matter how badly provoked, he would never physically harm a woman.

It was only the mean and cowardly, the *inadequate* men who took their anger out on someone weaker than themselves.

He came over to her and lifted her chin so that she was forced to look at him. 'Do as I say, Joanne,' he insisted quietly.

Blue eyes clashed with green.

For a moment she tried to stare him out, but his willpower proved stronger than hers. Her eyes were the first to drop and, her nerve suddenly cracking, she turned and fled.

When she had showered she brushed out her hair and swirled it on top of her head in an elegant chignon, before making up with care.

He wouldn't be able to accuse her of not trying to look her best, she thought with satisfaction. Though there was one thing that he seemed to have forgotten, and she had deliberately left it until the last minute to mention. She had absolutely nothing to wear to a party. Especially a posh one. And she had little doubt that it *would* be posh.

Rather than have her look totally out of place, he would be forced to let her stay behind.

There was a tap at the door, and his voice queried, 'How are you doing?'

'About ready.'

Pulling on her negligee, she went through to the living-room, where Brad, looking breathtakingly handsome in evening dress, was fastening his bow-tie.

As he glanced up she said sweetly, 'There's just one thing...I haven't got *anything* to wear.'

A knock cut through her words.

Brad opened the door, nodded his thanks and, passing over a fifty-krona tip in exchange for a package, closed it again.

Handing Joanne the large, flat box, he said calmly, 'How about this?'

With the infuriating knowledge that she had been out-manoeuvred, she put the box on the couch, tore off the silver and gold paper and removed the lid.

For a moment she stared down at the contents silently, then, with an odd tightness in her chest, lifted out the dress.

It was exquisite.

Ankle-length, and made of pure silk chiffon, it was the same deep blue as her eyes, and striking in its simplicity.

One shoulder was completely bare, while climbing over

the other, and running down the bodice to the thigh-length slit in the skirt, was a trail of small silver ivy leaves. There was a silver-lined matching wrap.

The designer label said simply: Tessin.

Never in her wildest dreams could she have afforded a dress like that.

'If you dig a little deeper,' Brad said, 'you should find some accessories.'

Beneath the dress there were silk stockings and gossamer undies, and to one side, carefully wrapped in tissue paper, a pair of silver sandals and a small evening purse.

How on earth had he managed to conjure up things like that on a Sunday? she wondered dazedly.

He answered her unspoken question. 'I have a friend who lives above her own boutique. Luckily it's just along the street...

'As there wasn't much time, having told Ingrid your size, I was forced to leave the shoes and undies to her. The only thing I personally chose was the dress. I hope you like it.'

Starting to realise the full implications, Joanne said stiltedly, 'It's beautiful, but I can't possibly accept such an expensive gift.'

'It isn't a gift. Nor is it for services rendered.' As the colour rose in her cheeks he went on, 'By the time this trip is over you'll have more than earned it...

'And I *do* mean for your secretarial skills,' he added sardonically.

Watching her soft lips tighten, he came over and took her hand, stroking the soft palm with his thumb. 'Please, Joanne, will you get dressed and come with me?'

Disconcerted because he'd *asked* rather than *ordered*, she took a steadying breath, and said, 'I don't understand why you want me.'

'For one thing Paul will be there, and I'd like you to meet him. For another, we have to consider poor Knut.'

'Poor Knut?' she echoed blankly.

'The young man Erika had in tow. He's been in love with her for a long time now, but I'm afraid she just uses him.'

'I don't see what difference *my* being there will make.'

'If I go alone, what do you think will happen?'

Put like that, Joanne had no doubt. It had been obvious at lunch time that, with Brad present, Knut came a very poor second.

Knowing full well that Erika would be anything but pleased, she squared her shoulders and agreed. 'Very well, I'll come.'

He used the hand he was still holding to draw her closer and, bending his head, kissed her lightly on the mouth. 'That's my girl.'

Her whole being made radiant by that fleeting kiss, she took the box and its contents through to the bedroom and put on her new finery as swiftly as possible.

Everything fitted to perfection. Which suggested a degree of experience on Brad's part that she preferred not to contemplate.

Settling the dress into place, she struggled to fasten the tiny, invisible hand-sewn hooks and eyes that ran down the back. She had managed to fasten two thirds of them, before admitting she would need Brad's help with the rest.

Stepping in front of the long mirror, she caught her breath, picturing her family's surprise at the transformation. Who would have thought she could look like this?

The beautiful material clung lovingly to the slender curves of hips and bust, but, though the bodice was daringly low, and she was bra-less, the dress was so well-cut that she felt completely at ease wearing it.

Well, *almost* completely.

Seeing how, when she moved, the skirt parted just enough to give a tantalising glimpse of a silk-clad leg, she thanked her lucky stars that her legs were in such good shape.

When, having gathered up her wrap and purse, she returned to the living-room, for what seemed an age Brad regarded her in silence.

Wondering if he was disappointed, she said hesitantly, 'I'm afraid I haven't any jewellery.'

With a slightly husky note in his voice, he assured her, 'You don't need any jewellery. It would be gilding the lily. You look absolutely stunning just as you are.'

Happiness and the warmth of his approval heady as vintage champagne, she said, 'I'm afraid I couldn't fasten all the hooks and eyes.'

'Then allow me.'

She turned her back.

They could have been a long-married husband and wife, she thought as with deft fingers he proceeded to complete the task.

But, as though to disprove that image, he lightly gripped her shoulders and, having touched his lips to the warmth of her nape, traced the exposed length of her spine with his tongue-tip.

Little shivers of excitement were still running through her as he turned her round and, saying, 'Mustn't spoil the lip gloss,' kissed the tip of her nose. Then, putting the wrap around her shoulders, he escorted her down to the waiting taxi.

Their destination was out of town, and during the drive, apparently deep in thought, Brad said nothing.

Joanne occupied her time by wondering what he was thinking, and worrying, just a little, about the coming evening.

The Reiersens' house was a huge old place situated at the top of a wooded incline. Blazing with lights, it was more like a castle than a house, Joanne decided as they left the road and wound their way up an imposing drive.

When their taxi stopped at a paved area crowded with cars Brad helped her out and, after a brief conversation with the driver, escorted her up a wide sweep of stone steps to a large, studded door.

He tugged on the bell-pull and the door was opened by a middle-aged manservant, who bowed his head politely and took Joanne's wrap.

As they made their way into the wood-panelled hall a waiter approached with a loaded tray, and Brad helped them both to a glass of champagne.

On their right, an archway led through to a large, chandelier-hung ballroom, where a crowd of people were gathered in laughing groups, sipping their drinks and talking.

It was a warm night, and on the far side of the room several pairs of French windows stood open, giving access to a lantern-lit terrace and garden.

On a raised dais, an orchestra was playing, and already several couples were dancing. Everyone appeared to be extremely well-dressed, the women wearing designer gowns and the men in immaculate evening clothes.

Joanne could only be pleased that at least she wouldn't look out of place.

They had just reached the archway and paused to survey the glittering scene, when a nice-looking man of medium height, with dark hair and a thin, intelligent face, made his way through the crowd to join them.

'Good to see you,' Brad greeted him.

The pair shook hands.

'Joanne, this is Paul Randall... Paul, my secretary, Joanne Winslow.'

Holding out her hand, she smiled. 'How do you do?'

For a moment he appeared nonplussed, then, his answering smile pleasant, he said, 'Nice to meet you, Miss Winslow... It *is* Miss Winslow?'

'Yes.'

As they shook hands he went on, 'Forgive me if I seem a bit confused. You see, I thought I knew Brad's secretary…small, ravishingly pretty, red-gold hair, bright blue eyes… I've even flirted with her…

'Now I find it's the same name, but a completely different girl…though equally beautiful,' he added gallantly.

When Brad stood, his face enigmatic, making no effort to explain, Joanne gathered herself and said steadily, 'Perhaps Mr Lancing should have introduced me as his *temporary* secretary. I'm just filling in for my sister.'

'Your sister? Oh, I see. You're not a bit alike…' Then with genuine concern, 'I do hope she isn't ill?'

'No, Milly's fine. It's just that she left, rather suddenly, to go to Scotland with her husband.'

'Her husband? When did she get married?'

'Last spring. Shortly after she started working for Lancing's.'

'Oh, I'm sorry.' He looked surprised. 'I didn't realise. She doesn't wear a wedding ring, and I've always known her as Miss Winslow.'

Frowning, Joanne was wondering why Milly hadn't worn her ring to work, when a tall, heavily built man with bushy eyebrows and a thatch of iron-grey hair appeared, and said, 'Glad you could come, Randall.'

'Thank you for inviting me,' Paul answered civilly as they exchanged handshakes.

Big and bluff and handsome, wearing impeccable evening dress, the newcomer looked to be in his late sixties or possibly early seventies.

'Brad, how are you?' He spoke excellent English, but with a slightly guttural accent.

'Very well… And you?'

'Starting to feel my age.'

The two men shook hands. Neither smiled.

There was a kind of careful cordiality there, Joanne realised, but no warmth.

An arm lightly encircling her waist, Brad drew her forward. 'Joanne, may I introduce Mr Reiersen... Harald, this is my secretary, Miss Winslow.'

'How do you do, Miss Winslow?'

Taking her hand, he smiled at her and, though the smile didn't reach his pale blue eyes, she recognised instantly that here was a man well-used to charming the ladies.

'How do you do?' she murmured, returning his smile.

Lifting the half-empty champagne glass he held, he toasted her. 'You look absolutely beautiful.'

More than a little uncomfortable under his admiring gaze, she said, 'Thank you.'

A waiter came hurrying up with a tray and, swapping his now empty glass for a full one, Reiersen turned again to Joanne and asked, 'How long are you intending to stay in Bergen?'

'I'm not really certain,' she answered carefully. 'It all depends on what Mr Lancing's plans are.'

His tone jocular, Reiersen admonished, 'Now, don't try to tell me that, as Brad's confidential secretary, you don't *know* what his plans are.'

Unsure what to say, she was relieved when Erika, dazzling in an aquamarine gown that shimmered when she moved, bore down on them.

'Brad, darling! So here you are at last. I've been watching out for you.' Then chidingly, 'You're so late I was starting to think you weren't going to come after all...'

She gave Joanne a cursory glance, before putting a possessive hand on Brad's arm and adding, 'Do come and dance with me.'

He hadn't moved when, doing a double take, Erika's ice-blue eyes swung back to Joanne.

Staring rudely, she said in a sharp voice, 'What an expensive-looking dress. Do tell me how you came by it. I'm sure you didn't buy *that* on the kind of wages a secretary earns.'

Feeling the hot colour rise in her cheeks, Joanne cursed

herself. Knowing the score, she should have been prepared for just that kind of remark.

Before she could find her voice, Brad cut in smoothly, 'As you've asked so nicely, my dear Erika, I'm quite sure Miss Winslow won't mind telling you where she got the dress.'

Joanne bit her lip. She certainly *did* mind. In fact she hadn't the slightest intention of admitting that she was wearing clothes Brad had paid for. Nor did she propose to lie.

Stepping into the breach, Paul said blandly, 'Perhaps you two girls can chat about clothes later? The orchestra has just started to play my favourite tune, and I was about to ask Miss Winslow to dance with me.'

Relieving Joanne of her glass, he set that and his own down on a side-table, and held out his hand to her. She took it gratefully and followed him onto the dance floor.

'It's an awful long time since I last danced,' she warned him as, clutching the evening purse in her left hand, she went into his arms.

'Dancing is like riding a bike, it's something you never forget how to do. And if you should happen to make a mistake it won't matter. I can assure you that while you're wearing that dress no one will be looking at your feet.'

Then quizzically, 'Does that make you feel better or worse?'

Smiling, she said, 'I'm not quite sure. But thank you for rescuing me.'

'Always at your service.' Then he added seriously, 'I presume you would have politely told that spoilt brat to mind her own business?'

'I'm just glad I didn't have to. It would have made it difficult for...everyone.'

'Brad in particular?'

'Well, yes.'

'There are times it would give me the greatest satisfaction to take that girl over my knee...

'Though I don't suppose I ever will,' he said regretfully. Adding with a grin, 'For one thing, she's bigger than me.'

Joanne gave a little choke of laughter.

'Seriously though, I often wonder how Brad puts up with her.'

'I don't suppose he comes to Norway very often.'

'Not all that often, but Erika stays in London a fair bit. Reiersen has a house near Hyde Park. He lived there for a number of years while his wife was ailing and needed specialised treatment.

'When they moved back to Bergen he kept the house, and shortly after Erika's marriage broke up he gave it to her...

'As you'll no doubt discover when you get to know them better, he absolutely dotes on her.'

'I take it she's an only child?'

'Can't you tell? And a late one, to boot. Apparently Reiersen waited years for a son and heir, and had given up hope of having any children.

'He was in his late forties by the time Erika was born, and after waiting so long for a child he was over the moon. Unfortunately his wife died while his daughter was still quite young, so she was all he had left.'

'That's sad,' Joanne said, feeling a quick sympathy for them both.

'I agree. She could well have turned out to be a much nicer person if it hadn't been for her father's influence...'

That was pretty much what Brad had said.

'In my opinion he's been the ruin of her. If he hadn't allowed her to marry that cousin of hers...'

'Perhaps he wasn't able to stop her.'

Paul shook his head. 'When she fell in lust with Lars he was about to marry someone else. Erika has always had everything she's ever wanted, so she appealed to her father…'

'But surely even he couldn't manipulate *people*—'

'That's just where you're wrong. Because that branch of the family have always been the poor relations, Daddy was able to buy his daughter the man of her choice by putting a vast amount of money into the company Lars was struggling to keep afloat.

'Of course, it suited him. Reiersen was hoping to groom his son-in-law to follow in his footsteps and be the son he never had.

'But I gather Lars soon got tired of playing the dutiful husband and, realising he'd sold his soul, opted out…'

As casually as possible Joanne asked, 'So what do you think she'll do now?'

'Erika's a very beautiful woman, and there's fire under that ice… If it wasn't for her father there would be plenty of men only too willing to chance getting burnt.'

There was something about the way he spoke that made her hazard, 'You amongst them?' Then quickly, 'I'm sorry, I shouldn't have said that.'

'Why not? We're having a very frank conversation. And yes, you're right, myself amongst them…'

The tune they were dancing to came to an end, and with scarcely a pause the band slipped into an old classic.

Paul's arm tightened around her, and as they moved off once more he continued, 'Believe me, I've no delusions about what kind of woman she is, and I wouldn't expect to change her overnight. But I do believe that with the right man…' He let the sentence tail off.

Curiously Joanne asked, 'How would you describe the right man?'

'In my opinion the right man would be someone strong, who genuinely loves her but isn't willing to spoil her rotten.

'The trouble is, she always seems to choose the wrong man.'

'You sound as if you think she's already chosen?'

'I'm fairly sure she has. But this time, if I'm any judge of character, she'll be on her own.'

'You're saying…?'

'I'm saying that on this occasion she may have set her sights on one of the few men Daddy won't be able to influence.'

CHAPTER EIGHT

'YOU mean Brad,' Joanne said flatly.

'Yes. As you may have noticed, she's crazy about him.'

Knowing she shouldn't, but doing it all the same, she asked, 'How do you think he feels about her?'

'Hard to say. Up till now, Brad has played it cool. He's not a man to wear his heart on his sleeve, so it's difficult to know which way he'll jump.

'He's always seemed fairly tolerant of her faults and failings...'

Remembering lunch time, and how he'd defended the blonde's rudeness, Joanne couldn't argue with that.

'If he *did* decide to take her on he's certainly strong enough, and I don't think he'd spoil her. But whether or not...'

As he was speaking she caught a glimpse of Erika and Brad on the far side of the dance floor. The blonde and he were closely entwined, her arms around his neck, her cheek resting against his.

Joanne felt such a stab of pain that she missed a step and stood on Paul's toe.

'Sorry,' she mumbled.

'That's all right,' he said, his eyes following hers before returning to her face.

Then thoughtfully, 'I guess we're both suffering from the same malady. But let's put our lacerated feelings aside and try to enjoy the rest of the evening... Oh, hell!'

'What's wrong?' she asked in alarm.

'Reiersen's heading this way, and I've noticed that he's been knocking it back a bit. I'm afraid he's always liked a spot too much of the bubbly...

'He may be going to ask you to dance, so if you don't want to take the risk, say so quickly, and I'll try to head him off while you run and hide in the loo.'

Suddenly liking this man enormously, she laughed and said, 'Thanks, but I think I'll take my chances on the dance floor. As I've already practically crippled you, I think Mr Reiersen is the one most at risk.'

'Nonsense,' Paul disagreed stoutly, 'when not distracted, you dance better than Erika.'

'I should hope so,' Reiersen remarked, appearing at their side. 'That daughter of mine has two left feet. That's why I take care not to dance with her.'

'I don't believe a word of it,' Joanne said lightly as they watched Brad and the blonde glide past.

'Elegance itself,' Paul commented.

Reiersen offered Joanne his hand. 'Shall we show them what we can do? You don't mind, Randall?'

'Not at all,' Paul said accommodatingly. 'I may try my luck with Erika.'

'I doubt if you'll get anywhere. She seems to prefer the partner she already has. Young Knut tried to cut in, and she soon sent him packing.'

'Oh, well, "Faint heart never won fair lady,"' Paul quoted cheerfully, and took himself off.

As though to confirm that Paul had been right in his assumption that Reiersen had been drinking, he moved clumsily and, catching Joanne's arm, knocked her purse from her hand.

'I'm so sorry,' he apologised, and stooped to pick it up.

'It's a bit of a nuisance,' she admitted. 'I should have left it somewhere.'

'Allow me.' He reached to put the small purse on a side-table.

'Thank you.'

Rather to Joanne's surprise, he proved to be a good

dancer, easy to follow, and light on his feet for so big a man.

As they moved round the floor, smiling and genial, he set himself out to charm her. 'Erika tells me you were lunching up Floyen. What did you think of the view from there?'

'I thought it was glorious,' she said sincerely.

'Then you like Bergen?'

'Oh, yes.'

'It was once Norway's largest city, and the undisputed capital of trade and shipping...'

Genuinely interested, she listened while he talked about Bergen's past. After a little while he paused to ask, 'Where are you staying?'

Startled by the abrupt change of subject, she answered, 'At Lofoten.'

'I understand Brad has a suite there?'

She said nothing, and after a moment Reiersen went on, 'Erika's fairly broad-minded about Brad paying for a little fun on the side, but she's keen that he should stay with her, as he has done in the past...'

The words coiled like a cold tentacle around Joanne's heart and squeezed, so that a sudden pain blotted out the rest of the sentence.

After a moment she recovered enough to hear Reiersen continuing, 'So you won't mind if he doesn't go back with you tonight?'

Realising he'd only asked her to dance in order to put this rather heavy-handed message across, she said, 'Not at all; I can always get a taxi,' and was pleased that her voice was steady.

'It may not be too easy to find a taxi. I happen to know there are several functions going on tonight, which means most taxi firms will already be fully booked.

'However, Randall is renting a house not far from

Lofoten, so I've no doubt he will be happy to take you back.'

'If Mr Randall can get a taxi, and he'll allow me, I'll be pleased to share it.'

'He came in his own car.'

Without thinking, she said, 'Oh, but I thought his car was off the road.'

'There was a spot of trouble with his brakes, I gather, but he's obviously had them fixed.

'Randall isn't the kind of young man to let grass grow under his feet. If he wasn't working for Brad *I* wouldn't mind employing him.' Almost to himself, he added, 'It didn't take him long to get on to Mussen…'

The name rang a distant bell, but before she could think why Reiersen was going on, 'But I'm talking too much, which is probably due to the fact that you're a very good listener…'

It was more probably due to the champagne, Joanne thought wryly.

After a moment or two of silence, his manner conspiratorial, he went on, 'I've heard a whisper that the DSL is having more trouble, including a fire in one of their hotels. Any idea what Brad's going to do about it? Is he considering calling in the police?'

'I'm afraid I don't know,' she said coolly.

'Suppose you have time to think about it? After all, there's such a thing as misplaced loyalty, and once Brad's had his fun…'

He left the sentence hanging in the air, but there was no mistaking his meaning.

There was a short pause, then he went on, 'I'm sure you're sensible enough to keep this conversation to yourself, and make any useful information pay big dividends.

'Perhaps you'll give an old man the pleasure of taking you out to lunch? Say tomorrow, or maybe the day after?'

Shaking her head, she said jerkily, 'I really don't think I'll be free…'

'That's a pity. I'd like to show you around the new leisure complex I've just had built. There are some wonderful shops in the arcade selling jewellery and clothes—'

'May I have my partner back?' Suddenly, like a knight in shining armour, Paul was there.

Just for an instant Reiersen looked ugly, then the geniality back, he said, 'Though I find it hard to part with her, how can I refuse?'

Releasing Joanne's hand, he added, 'If you should find you're free for lunch after all, just let me know.'

'Thank you, but I'm sure I won't be.'

Paul took her in his arms, and as they moved away she found her legs were distinctly wobbly.

When they were out of earshot he murmured, 'You were starting to look desperate, so I thought I'd better rescue you.'

'I can't tell you how grateful I am,' she said shakily.

'What did the old devil do? Make a pass?' As she shook her head he added, 'I thought he might have done when lunch was mentioned.'

'No. He'd heard a whisper that the DSL was having more trouble—'

'Now, where on earth did he hear that?' Paul sounded startled.

'He didn't say, but he did ask what Brad was doing about it. I told him I didn't know. Obviously believing I'm the kind of woman who can be bought, he hinted that if I gave him the information he wanted he'd make it worth my while…

'I don't understand why he approached me in this way, why he didn't just ask Brad,' she added helplessly.

'Perhaps he knows Brad wouldn't tell him.' Then thoughtfully, 'I presume he asked you to keep quiet?'

'His exact words were, ''I'm sure you're sensible enough

to keep this conversation to yourself, and make any useful information pay big dividends.'''

Paul nodded. 'I'm starting to realise that's the way Reiersen works. Though I imagine he's usually a lot more careful, and a better judge of character. It must be the drink that made him believe you could be bought.'

'I think it's more likely to be the dress,' she said evenly.

Diplomatically, Paul made no comment, and for a while they danced in silence, moving mechanically, each busy with their thoughts.

When the music came to an end and the doors into the adjoining room were opened Paul suggested, 'Shall we go and get some supper?'

Still feeling rattled, and with so much on her mind, Joanne wasn't very hungry, but she followed him through to where a long buffet table had been set up.

When they had helped themselves to a selection of delicious-looking food and a glass of wine they sat down at one of the small round tables that dotted the room.

There was no sign of either Erika or Brad, and to Joanne's great relief Reiersen too had vanished. Suddenly weary, she wished the evening were over.

But when it was she would be returning to Lofoten alone. She wondered bleakly why Brad had pressured her into coming in the first place if he was going to spend the *whole* evening with Erika. It made no sense...

'At least Reiersen puts on a good spread,' Paul remarked, breaking into her thoughts. 'That caviare is first class, some of the best I've ever tasted. Care to try some?'

She shook her head. 'I don't think so, thank you.'

'You don't seem to be eating much. Sure you're feeling all right?'

'Quite sure, thank you.'

Smothering a sigh, she picked up her fork and began to eat, tasting little, the expensive delicacies wasted on her as her whole mind focused on Brad.

In some ways he was a complete enigma. If Erika was already in Bergen, why had he needed a mistress as well as a secretary?

But maybe he hadn't...

What if, because of his reputation, she had made a mistake? Jumped to the wrong conclusions? Perhaps he had never *intended* her to sleep with him?

But in that case, why had he let...no, *encouraged* her to believe he did?

All at once it was painfully obvious.

Thinking about her behaviour, the names she had called him, the way she had smacked his face, she realised that forcing her to come with him, *making her think the worst,* had simply been his way of getting even.

Now she was looking at it from a slightly different perspective, she could see clearly that he had never *meant* to sleep with her. If he had he would have come through to the bedroom rather than making up the couch.

He hadn't needed her. *She* had needed him.

She recalled all too clearly how she had gone looking for him, how he'd said, 'As you've come to me, I guess we can do something about it...'

Then later, when he'd taken her back to bed, he hadn't slept beside her. He'd gone back to his solitary couch.

Which said everything.

Feeling a burning sense of shame, she realised that she had made a complete fool of herself. He had probably felt sorry for her, been amused by her lack of experience, laughed at her gullibility...

Don't get mad, get even.

Well, he had made her pay for her stupidity. Got even. That being the case, she could no longer believe he would carry out his threat to ruin Steve, so tomorrow she would get the first flight possible back to London...

'Do you want anything else?' Paul asked. 'A sweet, or some coffee?'

Feeling slightly sick, she shook her head. 'No, thanks.'

'Then shall we return to the fray?'

As she rose he urged, 'Cheer up; you look as if you're about to climb the steps to the guillotine.'

Though she couldn't admit it, she was experiencing something of the same despair.

'Paul,' she asked impulsively, 'how long were you planning to stay tonight?'

'Not too long. Why? Oh, don't worry, if Brad hasn't put in an appearance I'll stay as long as you need me.'

'Thank you, you're an angel...but I was going to ask, when you *do* go, could I beg a lift with you?'

'Of course. Though surely Brad will—'

'Mr Reiersen told me Brad will be going home with...' She broke off suddenly, realizing she might be about to hurt him.

'With Erika?' Paul hazarded. 'Well, if you take my advice, you won't believe all Reiersen tells you. I've discovered that he's adept at manipulating people.'

When they returned to the glittering ballroom the band leader was just making an announcement in Norwegian.

'This is a traditional lovers' waltz,' Paul translated as couples began to crowd onto the floor.

A lovers' waltz... In her mind's eye, she could see Erika and Brad dancing together, closely entwined...

It shouldn't matter, she thought fiercely.

But it did.

Seeing her face, Paul urged, 'Come on, don't look so tense. It's nowhere near as complicated as it may first appear, and you can keep the same partner.'

Her stomach tied in knots, she had started to shake her head, when Brad appeared from nowhere and said firmly, 'Our dance, I think.'

He had just taken her hand, when Erika came storming up and spoke to him in Norwegian.

He replied evenly, in English, 'The last time I saw you you were dancing with Knut.'

'I don't want to dance this one with Knut,' she said urgently. 'I was saving it specially for you.'

'Sorry, but I've just asked Miss Winslow to be my partner.'

'If you *must* dance with her, surely you can leave it until later?'

'I'm afraid not.'

'Please, Brad...' Seeing her appeal was having no effect, she said furiously, 'How could you? You know perfectly well that this is a lovers' waltz.'

She had raised her voice, and heads were starting to turn.

'Then we mustn't waste it.' An arm around her waist, Paul swept Erika onto the floor.

When she began to protest he stopped in his tracks, turned her towards him and, holding her upper arms, said something quietly.

After a moment he released her and, stepping back, held out his hand, unsmiling.

Looking shaken, and oddly vulnerable, she took it, and together they joined the throng of dancers.

'She may well have met her match there,' Brad remarked. Then, putting an arm around Joanne's waist, 'Let's dance.'

Why had he insisted on dancing with *her* rather than his girlfriend? Joanne wondered as he led her onto the floor. Perhaps he was using these tactics to bring the blonde to heel? Emphasising who was master?

If he was she shouldn't be allowing him to use her, shouldn't be playing his rotten game. But she loved him so much that she had been unable to forgo this last chance of being held in his arms...

She loved him so much...

Deciding that what she felt for Brad was a purely physical thing, she had called it lust rather than love. But all the time her subconscious had known the truth. It was love.

And love brought such pain. If Erika truly loved him she could find it in her heart to be sorry for the girl…

The orchestra started to play and, smiling down at her, Brad took her in his arms, making her whole body come alive with longing.

Suddenly terrified that he would realise how she was feeling, she looked anywhere but at him as they began to waltz.

'Relax,' he said in her ear. 'You were moving much more easily when you were dancing with Paul.'

Dancing with Paul hadn't affected her, so she had been *able* to relax.

Brad's arm tightened a little, drawing her closer, and he bent his dark head to put his cheek against hers. He moved with a lithe masculine grace that made him easy to follow and a pleasure to dance with.

She reminded herself that this would be the only time she would ever get to dance with him. If she wasted this chance she would regret it forever.

Giving herself up to the sheer pleasure of being in his arms, feeling the slight roughness of his cheek against hers, she let the tenseness drain out of her and her body melt against his.

They had circled the dance floor a couple of times, when he said in her ear, 'Unless you want to change partners, which is allowed at this point, keep hold of my hand.'

With an awful feeling that Erika might still claim him, she held tightly to his hand as the dancers parted to form parallel lines.

Amid much laughter and good-natured banter, some part-ner-swapping took place, but Joanne was reassured by a glimpse of Erika and Paul further down the line, and still hand in hand.

The lines of dancers, still holding hands and moving in unison, circled the ballroom before forming into sets.

At the end of each figure, the couples raised linked right hands above their heads and, smiling, faced each other through the arch.

When the last movement was completed Brad's left arm drew her closer and, smiling into her eyes, he bent to kiss her.

She should have been prepared, but she wasn't. The flood of feeling that swept over her left her clinging to him as a drowning person might cling to a rock.

His lips still lingered when most of the other couples were drawing apart, and when he finally lifted his head she was dazed and confused.

Out of the sea of faces, she became aware that Erika's burning gaze was fixed on them, and her father was standing close by, apparently waiting to talk to Brad.

Pulling herself free, she fled.

There was no sign of Paul and, feeling an urgent need to escape, she made her way through the nearest French windows and onto the terrace, which seemed to be deserted.

The air, though appreciably cooler than it had been, was still far from cold. Finding a corner furthest away from the lights, she sank down on a wrought-iron bench and looked blindly out over the moonlit garden.

So much had happened over the past three days, making her feel so many things she had never imagined herself feeling. Turning her world upside-down. Altering her life.

Tomorrow she would go back to her everyday existence and do her best to pick up the threads. But she already knew that nothing would ever be the same again.

Still, at least she had *lived*. She knew what it was like to love a man, to feel passion and rapture and jealousy— oh, yes, she was as bitterly jealous of Erika as the blonde was of her—to be truly *alive*.

No one could ever take that away from her. And though

her love was misplaced and foolish, and had brought almost as much pain as pleasure, it was still the most wonderful thing that had ever happened to her. A gift to be cherished.

If she sometimes found herself longing for what might have been, she wouldn't harbour regrets. She was one of the lucky ones. Some people grew old without ever knowing real love. As she would have done if she hadn't met Brad…

A movement caught her eye, and she turned her head to see the tall figure of a man strolling across the terrace towards her.

Though his back was to the light, his face in shadow, she would have known him from a million other men. Known that easy carriage and the tilt of his dark head…

'So this is where you're hiding,' Brad said.

Somehow she found her voice, and denied, 'I'm not hiding. I just needed a breath of fresh air.'

'Would you like to dance any more?'

'No… No, thank you.' Then hopefully, 'Is Paul ready to leave?'

'What has Paul got to do with it?'

'Well, I…I asked him if he'd give me a lift back.'

'I thought you two were getting on well,' Brad remarked coldly. 'But when I take a woman out I make a point of seeing her home.'

'Oh, but I—'

'I'm afraid you've missed your chance to change partners, which means you're stuck with me. So if you're ready to go?'

As she rose to her feet he added, 'We have a very early start tomorrow.'

She took a deep breath, and blurted out, 'I intend to go home tomorrow.'

'Do you, now?' he said grimly. 'What about your brother? Or have you decided you don't care what happens to his company?'

'Of course I care what happens to it.'

'Then I shall expect you to stick to our bargain.'

'If your intention is just to use me to bring your girlfriend to heel—'

'What makes you think that?' he broke in.

'Well, isn't that why you insisted on dancing with me? Why you kissed me the way you did? Because Erika was watching?'

'Is Erika watching now?'

'No...'

Pulling her into his arms, he kissed her with a punitive thoroughness that left her breathless.

Then, letting her go so suddenly that she staggered, he informed her curtly, 'That's just to prove I find you quite kissable enough not to need the kind of underhand motive you've credited me with...

'Now, if you're quite ready? Our taxi should be here. I've already thanked our host and hostess, and said our goodnights to them and to Paul...'

Joanne could only be thankful for that.

His hand beneath her elbow, he escorted her back through the press of people in the ballroom, and across the hall.

A word to a hovering attendant produced her wrap, and a moment later Brad was helping her into the waiting taxi.

The journey back to Lofoten was a silent one. Brad, his face set, stared straight ahead, while Joanne struggled to get her chaotic thoughts into some kind of order.

Without success.

The only thing that seemed to matter was that she wasn't going home tomorrow after all. The only thing she could feel was joy. She would see him, hear his voice, be with him for a little longer.

But on what terms?

He had insisted, 'I shall expect you to stick to our bargain...'

That *bargain* was still fresh in her mind.

When she had said, 'I won't be your mistress,' he had answered, 'If you really want to save your brother, you'll be anything I want you to be.'

So where did that leave her?

She hadn't the faintest idea.

But one thing she was certain about, knowing he hadn't *intended* to make her his mistress, she wouldn't go to him…

Her thoughts were interrupted by the taxi drawing up outside Lofoten. When Brad had helped her out and paid the driver, without touching her he escorted her across the smoothly pebbled frontage.

She could sense his pent-up anger simmering just beneath the surface, and this time she went in without a glance at the dragons.

As they crossed the lobby he paused to ask a young, fresh-faced man at the night-desk to have a pot of coffee and a plate of sandwiches sent up to their suite.

'Straight away, Mr Lancing,' the youth answered smartly.

He was as good as his word.

By the time Brad had taken Joanne's wrap, removed his own jacket and tie, and rolled up his sleeves to riddle the stove and pile on more logs, a knock announced the arrival of their supper.

Brad took the tray with a word of thanks, and set it down on the long table. Then, indicating the couch, he asked ironically, 'Won't you join me?'

Joanne, who had been hovering uncertainly, went to sit down, taking care to keep her distance. The skirt of her dress parted, exposing a silk-clad knee and shapely thigh.

She hastily rearranged it.

Smiling wolfishly, he queried, 'Coffee?'

'Please.'

He poured two cups, and put one in front of her before offering her a sandwich.

'No, thank you,' she refused politely.

'Have you had anything to eat tonight?'

'Yes. Paul and I went through to the buffet.' Hoping to get back on an amicable footing, she went on, 'He remarked that the caviare was some of the best he'd ever tasted. What did you think?'

'I didn't get to eat,' Brad replied brusquely. 'And before you jump to conclusions, I wasn't with Erika all the time. I was talking to Reiersen.'

It had been an emotionally fraught evening; upset by his coldness, and feeling the sudden prick of tears behind her eyes, she said huskily, 'Brad...I'm sorry if you're angry with me...'

He sighed. 'Forgive me if I've seemed short with you, but I don't take kindly to being brushed aside for another man, not even Paul.'

'B-but I thought you were going home with Erika,' she stammered.

'What on earth gave you that idea?'

'Mr Reiersen told me she wanted you to.'

Frowning a little, he suggested, 'Perhaps you'd better tell me exactly what Reiersen said to you.'

'He said, ''Erika's fairly broad-minded about Brad paying for a little fun on the side.'''

As she paused to try and steady her voice Brad said, 'Presumably the ''paying for a little fun on the side'' is a reference to the dress. But do go on.'

Her voice under control once more, she continued, 'Then he added, ''But she's keen that he should stay with her, as he has done in the past. So you won't mind if he doesn't go back with you tonight?'''

'I see,' Brad said slowly. 'Of course, I've always known that Reiersen's not above lying and trying to manipulate people, to achieve his own ends...'

Paul had said much the same.

'Or Erika's, for that matter. He'd do anything to get his daughter what she wants.'

'And she wants you,' Joanne said flatly.

'I won't deny that she gave me a very pressing invitation to go home with her and stay. An invitation I declined. Which didn't please her.

'That's probably why Reiersen found it necessary to try and make trouble.'

When Joanne just looked at him he assured her. 'I have *never* stayed with Erika. The only time we've ever slept under the same roof was at Reiersen's house one night last winter.

'She was living at home after the break-up of her marriage, and I'd been invited to talk business over dinner. A blizzard blew up, and Reiersen offered me a bed for the night. So I slept there. Alone.'

Joanne felt such a rush of gladness and gratitude that, afraid he'd see, she looked away.

'I presume you think I'm lying?'

Turning to face him, she said, 'No. I don't think you're lying. Though there's no need to explain yourself to me.'

'Does that mean you don't care whether I've slept with Erika or not?'

'It means I don't consider it's any of my business.'

'In the normal state of things, what happened before I met you wouldn't be. But this is a little different, so I prefer to set matters straight.'

Sardonically, he added, 'I'm getting more than a little tired of being misjudged.'

'I'm sorry, truly I am, but with your...' Too late she stopped herself.

'Reputation?' he suggested.

Flushing, she said, 'Well, you have to admit it isn't a good one.'

Looking quietly furious, he said, 'I don't have to admit

anything of the kind. The only people who think badly of me in that respect seem to be you and your brother. Though I haven't lived like a monk, I'm certainly no Casanova.'

Angry in her turn, she demanded, 'Then how do you explain trying to seduce an eighteen-year-old married woman?'

A white line appearing round his mouth, he said, 'No matter what lies your sister may have told you, in the past I've always left married women and other men's fiancées strictly alone. And I can honestly say that, so far as I know, no woman has been worse off for knowing me.'

'I suppose you mean *financially*?' Looking down at the dress, she said caustically, 'I certainly can't deny you're generous.'

He made a sudden movement, and, realising she'd gone too far, she flinched away.

'You're quite safe,' he informed her icily. 'It isn't my style to strike a woman. All the same, it might be as well if you went to bed.'

Wanting to weep, because she hadn't meant it to be like this, she got to her feet and went blindly out of the room.

Closing the bedroom door behind her, she hovered helplessly, feeling sick and shaken. When her intention had simply been to apologise, how could such an ugly quarrel have flared?

But somehow it had. And it was very largely her fault. She hadn't meant to bring up his reputation, nor taunt him with the dress.

If only she had been more careful, guarded her tongue instead of saying the things she had, it could have been so different.

After all, he had chosen to come back to Lofoten with her, rather than go with Erika, and he had taken the trouble to deny the lie Reiersen had told her.

Would he listen if she went back and told him she was sorry?

No, after last night she couldn't bring herself to go back in there. He was bound to think the worst. In any case, it was too late. Too much damage had been done.

A cold space around her heart, she knew she had spoilt whatever chance there might have been of putting things right between them.

And no matter what he was, what kind of reputation he had, she loved him. Completely. Hopelessly.

In the past she had sometimes wondered how sensible women could choose to love, and keep on loving, totally unsuitable men.

Now she knew. It wasn't something one *chose* to do, it just happened, and there was no help for it.

All the unaccustomed emotion, the passion, the jealousy, the despair that she had been feeling suddenly became too much. Overwrought, she sank down on the bed and, burying her face in the pillow, began to sob uncontrollably.

CHAPTER NINE

HER misery was so great that she failed to hear either the tap, or the door being opened, just Brad's voice saying gently, 'Come on, now, there's no need to cry like that.'

Gulping, she sat up and, tears running down her face in tracks of shiny wetness, mumbled, 'I'm not crying.'

'As that statement is patently a lie, I shall ignore it.' He was wearing a short, dark silk robe and his hair was still a little damp from the shower.

'But why weep all over the pillow when I've got a perfectly good shoulder?'

He held out his arms, and like someone going home she went into them.

Now, rather than despair, she shed tears of relief, while his hand moved up and down her spine in a soothing gesture almost as old as time.

After a while, when her sobs had lessened, he queried, 'About done?'

Sniffing, she lifted her head and reluctantly moved out of his arms. He produced a folded handkerchief and handed it to her.

'Thank you.' She sat on the nearest chair and, scrubbing at her face, went on unsteadily, 'I'm sorry… I didn't mean to quarrel with you. I shouldn't have said what I did. I would have come back and told you so, but I thought you might think…'

A gleam of amusement in his eyes, he queried, 'And if I had thought what you imagined I might think, what would you have done?'

'Felt ashamed…after last night,' she added awkwardly.

'It's perfectly natural to want a man…'

She didn't just *want* him, she *needed* him, as she needed air to breathe.

'So why feel ashamed?'

'I thought you might not have wanted me.'

'How can you doubt it?'

'You didn't *plan* to make love to me.'

When he made no effort to deny it, she sighed. 'You didn't need to, when Erika was already here and more than willing.'

'It had nothing to do with Erika.'

'But you didn't want to make love to me. If you had, you wouldn't have made up the couch.'

'You're wrong about my not wanting to make love to you. I wanted to very much. But no matter what you may believe about me, I've never taken a woman who was remotely unwilling...

'I thought you *might* want me, but I couldn't be sure. So I decided to let you make the first move.'

'And if I hadn't?'

'You would still be a virgin.'

Feeling the hot colour rise in her cheeks, she bit her lip. Since meeting Brad her usual cool control had totally deserted her.

Instead of behaving like the modern woman she was, she had acted as though she were in some Victorian melodrama, she thought crossly. She had fluttered and palpitated, blushed and cried. The only thing left to do was to swoon or get the vapours.

And she had no intention of doing either.

'Well, I can't say I'm sorry not to be a twenty-five-year-old virgin,' she said crisply. 'There's something almost laughable about the idea.'

'I don't think so,' he disagreed soberly. 'Even in today's world, virginity is a precious gift, often parted with much too lightly. Or simply thrown away...

'And you're not twenty-five until tomorrow.'

'How do you know it's tomorrow?'

'I heard your birthday mentioned, and I asked your brother when it was. He told me with the greatest reluctance. He seemed to think I would use the occasion to ply you with diamonds and have my wicked way with you...'

While he was speaking the clock in the living-room chimed twelve.

Greatly daring, she asked, 'And are you going to?'

He shook his head regretfully. 'I'm afraid I forgot to buy any diamonds, and I've already had my wicked way with you.

'However, once I've unfastened your dress, which is what I came in to do, I might want to have it all over again.'

'Only *might*?'

'Intend?'

'That's better.' Then, catching sight of her ravaged face in the mirror, 'Or perhaps you don't want me all swollen-eyed and blotchy?'

He stooped to kiss her pink and puffy eyelids. 'I want you any way I can get you.'

Suddenly needing to know, she asked, 'Brad...last night...why did you go back to sleep on the couch?'

Standing looking down at her, he answered, 'It occurred to me that in the cold light of day you might change your mind and wish the whole thing had never happened.

'If that had been the case it could have come as a nasty shock waking up to find a man you regard as a lecher lying beside you.'

She winced. But then, she had asked for it. Taking a deep breath, she pleaded, 'You will stay with me tonight?'

'If you want me to. But if you think you might have regrets in the morning, you'd better tell me now.'

She could feel her pulse beating in her throat and wrists as she answered, 'I won't have any regrets.'

*　*　*

When they were both naked in bed he rolled over and held himself above her, looking down into her face. 'You're sure about this?' he asked.

'Quite sure,' she assured him huskily. And, on fire for him, begged, 'Please don't make me wait.'

He didn't. His lovemaking intense, focused, direct, he carried her to the heights until, like a sky-rocket, the spiralling ecstasy he was engendering exploded in a shower of golden stars.

Lying beneath him, she enjoyed the weight of his dark head on her breast, the feel of his body against hers, until their heart-rate and breathing had returned to something approaching normal.

She was waiting for him to lift himself away and draw her close, when, raising his head, he said, 'That was specially to please you.'

'It did.'

'Well, now I'm going to please you a whole lot more.'

Completely sated, she said contentedly, 'That's not possible. At least at the moment.'

'We'll see, shall we?' Rolling over and taking her with him, so that his body was supporting hers, he put his hands either side of her ribcage and, his arms propped on his elbows, lifted her.

She gasped as his tongue laved a nipple before he drew it into his mouth and, tugging a little, began to suck, sending the most exquisite sensations darting through her.

Immediately, the hunger she had thought was more than satisfied sprang to life, demanding to be appeased.

Lowering her, he turned again, so that she was lying on her back and he was stretched out beside her. Then, nuzzling his face against her breasts, he slid his hand between the warm, velvet skin of her inner thighs.

Her breath was coming in shallow gasps when he paused in his administrations to ask, 'Still think it's not possible?'

'No.'

His voice full of satisfaction, he queried, 'Then I take it you'd like me to go on?'

He was so sure of himself, so *complacent* that she wanted to shake him by saying no, but somehow she found herself saying weakly, 'Yes, please.'

This time his lovemaking was lazily assured, wonderfully inventive, and teasing to the point of near-madness. He knew exactly where to touch to drive her wild, to have her shuddering and begging…

When at length she could stand no more he sent her tumbling and spinning into the abyss, before settling her head on his shoulder, and saying, 'Sleep now. We need to set off quite early in the morning.'

Joanne awoke to find they had been sleeping on their sides, knees bent and lying spoon-fashion. Her back was against Brad's chest, her buttocks resting on his thighs. The weight of his arm lay across her ribs, and his chin pressed lightly on the top of her head.

She could feel the strong beat of his heart, and the rise and fall of his chest as he breathed. Filled with an utter and complete contentment, she gave silent thanks to whatever gods look after the happiness of mere mortals.

'Good morning,' he said.

'How did you know I was awake?'

'Your breathing altered.'

Daylight was just starting to filter through the greeny-blue curtains, and the room had the dimly lit quiet of an underwater cave. 'What time is it?' she asked idly.

'Time I was making a move. The car I hired will be arriving soon, and we still have to eat breakfast.'

Watching him climb out of bed, and admiring the lean elegance of his body as he pulled on his robe, she stirred herself. 'Then I'd better—'

Drawing back the curtains, he said, 'Stay where you are. It's breakfast in bed for the birthday girl.'

'It sounds very decadent. I don't ever recall having breakfast in bed before.'

'Well, you know what they say about trying everything once?'

Settling back against the pillows, she asked curiously, 'Why do we need to get off so early?'

'As a special present I'm taking you to see the Briksdal, and it's a fair distance away.'

'The Briksdal? What's that?'

'If you don't know then we'll keep it as a surprise.'

'What sort of clothes should I wear?'

'Something casual. A shirt and jeans would do fine. Oh, and sensible shoes… We'll be staying overnight, so you'll need to pack a bag… Ah, this sounds like breakfast.'

When he returned wheeling a trolley covered with a white cloth, she was sitting, black hair tumbling around her shoulders, the duvet pulled up high enough to hide her breasts and tucked modestly beneath her arms.

Having brought the trolley to the bedside, Brad spread his palms for her inspection, and intoned, 'Nothing in my hands, nothing up my sleeves…' Then, with a grin, he whipped off the cloth and, like a magician producing a rabbit from a hat, produced a posy of fresh flowers and handed them to her.

'Happy birthday.'

Flushing with pleasure, she buried her nose in their scented freshness. 'Thank you, they're lovely.' Impulsively, she added, 'Much better than diamonds.'

'A lot of women would find that debatable,' he countered drily.

Sitting on the edge of the bed, he handed her what was clearly a birthday card, though in Norwegian.

He had written a few words on it, but, as they too were in Norwegian, the only thing she could decipher was his name.

The picture was of a male elk with a soppy grin on its

face, handing a bunch of flowers to a female elk with inch-long eyelashes.

It was so ridiculous that she started to laugh. When she stopped laughing she asked, 'What does it say?'

'I'm not sure if the wording's appropriate. Perhaps I'll tell you when I've known you longer.'

His words reminded her that, though she was closer to him than she had ever been to any man, it was only four days since they'd met.

It was a strange and sobering thought.

'Now last, but not least…' He handed her a package no bigger than her thumb.

She tore off the paper and once more began to laugh helplessly.

The small wooden figure, which was dressed in a jerkin and boots, was grotesquely ugly, with long wisps of griz-zled hair, a wart, and a huge hooked nose and pointed chin which almost met.

'What on earth is it?' she managed.

Straight-faced, he told her, 'A lucky troll. His name's Olaf. As you're a woman of discerning taste, I'm sure you'll get to love him.'

'I do already. I'll take him with me everywhere.' Then impulsively, 'Thank you; I don't know when I've had so much fun on a birthday.'

'The day's hardly started, so hopefully there's lots more to come.

'Now for some breakfast…'

He helped her to a bowl of something resembling muesli mixed with delicious wild berries, then a kind of toasted croissant filled with a mixture of smoked ham and creamy cheese.

Wiping her buttery fingers on a napkin, she murmured, 'Mmm…delicious,' and reached to replace the empty plate.

The movement exposed one shapely pink-tipped breast.

Feeling ridiculously shy, she used her left hand to re-anchor the duvet.

He sighed and, cocking an eyebrow at her, asked hopefully, 'You don't think you're in any danger of putting on weight?'

Remembering their conversation over brunch at the airport, she said, 'No. As I told you, I have the kind of metabolism that burns off fat... In any case,' she added firmly, 'I'm getting plenty of...exercise.'

'You can never have too much of a good thing.'

'I could...after a meal like that.'

Leaning forward, he whispered a suggestion in her ear that made her blush rosily.

'I thought you said we needed to be off early.'

He dropped a light kiss on her lips and remarked mockingly, 'You're starting to sound just like a wife.'

Though she knew perfectly well that this was a brief affair, nothing more, nothing less, she felt such a tug at her heartstrings that her eyes filled with tears.

Luckily he had turned away without noticing.

Less than an hour later, casually dressed in well-cut trousers, a fine polo-necked sweater and a light jacket, Brad helped a similarly-dressed Joanne into the four-wheel-drive he had hired.

As soon as he had stowed their overnight bags, he tossed a picnic hamper in beside them and slid behind the wheel. Within minutes they were heading north-east out of Bergen and into central fjord country.

The day was golden and glorious. Fluffy cotton-wool clouds hung motionless in a sky of cornflower-blue, while early-morning sunshine warmed the grey rocks and brought the reds and golds of autumn to glowing life.

'Isn't it gorgeous weather?' she remarked.

He gave her a smiling sideways glance, and, his green eyes dancing, told her, 'I ordered it specially for you.'

They were soon travelling through scenery that was truly magnificent, with towering snow-capped mountains, deep-blue fjords, picturesque woodland and waterfalls that ranged from delicate plumes, fine as spun silk, to raging cataracts.

Joanne sat silent and awestruck, poignantly aware that she had never been so happy in her life.

Though in places the road surface was dusty and full of potholes, the sturdy jeep made light work of the rough and mountainous terrain, and they were approaching their destination by lunch time.

'Won't be long now,' Brad told her as, leaving the road, they began to follow a narrow track through wooded country.

When they reached a wide clearing he stopped the car and said, 'This is where we use other means of transport.'

The 'other means of transport' was a string of ponies and traps drawn up beneath the shade of the overhanging trees. All the traps were black and Victorian-looking, their green hoods folded neatly back. The ponies were light tan-coloured, with creamy tails and manes.

He lifted a hand, and the driver at the head of the queue detached his vehicle from the rest and came ambling over.

Brad helped Joanne into the high, open carriage, and, having tossed up the picnic basket, joined her on the wooden seat.

The driver mounted with the agility of a monkey, and turned to give them a gap-toothed grin. A wizened-walnut of a man, with wispy grey hair and a big, hooked nose, he was so like Olaf that, catching Brad's eye and seeing the unholy gleam there, Joanne was hard put to it not to laugh.

Her bottom lip caught in her teeth, she looked resolutely away as the driver chirruped to the pony, and they started at a leisurely trot up a fairly steep path.

They had gone about a mile when they came to a tremendous gorge, where a spectacular waterfall plunged down the rocks and disappeared into the depths.

Spanning the chasm was a frail wooden bridge which seemed to shake beneath the thunderous onslaught of the water. Spray was flung high into the air, drenching everything in a rainbow cloud.

Turning, the driver pulled the hood over their heads, before urging the pony into a gallop.

They were shaken and thrown about as the trap bumped and rattled over the uneven planking, and when Brad put his arms around her Joanne clung to him tightly, half laughing, half afraid of the abyss beneath their feet.

As though reaching for the sky, the road climbed even higher, and after a word with the driver they left the trap and, with Brad carrying the picnic basket, began to walk.

When they reached the edge of the trees he put the basket down, and, with one hand over Joanne's eyes and the other cupping her elbow, urged her a few steps.

'Now look.'

She gasped in wonder.

An awe-inspiring glacier filled the end of the narrow valley like a massive pile of sparkling candy sugar. Pale blue fissures scarred its rough surface, and as she watched an enormous piece broke away with an ear-splitting crack.

'So this is Briksdal?' she breathed.

'Yes. It's the most accessible arm of the Jostedal glacier.'

'I've never seen a real glacier before.'

'Well, if you want a closer look, there are guides who take tours over the safe parts, but we'll have to leave that until we come again.'

Until we come again... The words wrapped themselves warmly around her heart.

Below the giant ice fall, water flowed from a tunnel it had cut for itself through the slow-moving mass. Despite the heat of the day, large chunks of ice floated in the clear aquamarine water of the lake like miniature bergs.

Completely entranced by the spectacle, Joanne stood motionless until Brad picked up the basket and led the way along the side of the lake.

He chose a grassy bank in the sun, and, having discarded his jacket, opened the basket, put a blanket down to sit on, and spread out the picnic.

Enjoying the pine-scented air, the sunshine and the lovely view, they sipped a glass of white wine and began to eat in companionable silence.

Then, opening a small container of gleaming black caviare, Brad spread some onto a tiny biscuit and popped it into her mouth, enquiring, 'Is this as good as the one Paul praised?'

Wondering why he'd brought that up, she ate the morsel before answering, 'I'm afraid I don't know. I didn't try it.'

His voice even, he went on, 'You saw quite a lot of my right-hand man. What did you think of him?'

Recalling how he had said, 'I don't take kindly to being brushed aside for another man, not even Paul,' she hesitated, before admitting, 'I liked him very much.'

If it hadn't been so ridiculous, she might have suspected Brad was jealous as, his jaw tightening, he said a shade curtly, 'That was the impression I got.'

'I was grateful he took pity on me, otherwise I would have been alone.'

With a sigh, Brad reached for her hand and lifted it to his lips. 'I'm sorry I neglected you. But Reiersen wanted to talk business, and I felt it was important to hear what he had to say.'

To her great relief he let the matter drop, and after a moment became his old relaxed self again.

When they had finished tucking into the food they shared a flask of coffee before repacking the basket. Then, Brad's arm around her shoulders, and their backs against an outcrop of smooth grey rock, they lifted their faces to the warmth of the sun.

Contented and at ease, totally relaxed once more, Joanne closed her eyes, and in a moment or two she slept, a deep, quiet sleep that, after so much emotional turmoil, was curiously healing.

After a while she dreamt Brad was kissing her, softly, sweetly… When he began to draw away, afraid that he was going to leave her, she clutched at his sweater, muttering, 'No, no…'

'Wake up, Sleeping Beauty.'

The teasing words wrenched her back to consciousness and the realisation that she had been sound asleep, cradled in the crook of his arm.

Sitting up straight, she said, 'I'm sorry.'

'There's no need to be sorry.' He was looking at her, an expression on his face that could have been mistaken for tenderness. 'It seemed a shame to disturb you, but the sun's going down and we ought to be getting back.'

'How long have I…?'

'Almost two hours.'

'Two hours!' she exclaimed.

'You must have needed it, so regard it as therapy.'

The air was appreciably cooler now, and she reached for her jacket.

As Brad helped her into it she noticed he moved his right arm awkwardly, and wondered how long he had been enduring the pain of cramp, rather than disturb her.

As soon as he had replaced the blanket and fastened the lid of the wicker basket, they set off back to where the pony and trap were waiting.

'Thank you,' she said simply when he'd helped her into the trap and jumped in beside her. 'It's been a perfect day.'

Slanting her a glance, he reminded her, 'And the night is still to come.'

'Where are we spending the night?'

'At a little town called Lanadal. It's about an hour's drive away. Rather than one of the larger, newer hotels, I thought it would be fun to stay at Trollfoss, a small place that used to be a private house.

'It was built in the Victorian era, and what it lacks in modern amenities it makes up for in character. The beds are large and comfortable, with brass bedsteads and feather mattresses. I think you'll like it.'

'I'm sure I will,' she said contentedly.

The small, picturesque town of Lanadal lay at the foot of a hill and straddled a shallow, fast-flowing river that tumbled over a rocky bed.

By the time they drove through its narrow cobbled streets lined with colourful timber houses, it was dusk and the old-fashioned streetlights were adding an almost Dickensian atmosphere.

Trollfoss stood alone on the outskirts of town and partway up the hill. Built of clapboard and painted green, it was topped with gables and turrets, spires and curlicues.

When they drew up on the lantern-lit forecourt, and Brad helped her out, Joanne laughed with delight. Peering down from a niche above the door was a large child-sized replica of a troll.

'I thought you could introduce Olaf to his namesake,' Brad told her with a grin.

'I did wonder about the name Trollfoss,' she said.

Lifting out their overnight bags, he explained, 'You can't see them from this side of the house, but if you listen the muted roar in the background is the Troll Falls.'

Once inside, she saw that the hotel, as Brad had said, was very Victorian, with rich red carpets, heavily framed pictures, velvet, gold-tassled curtains and a riot of filigree carving.

At the polished desk was an elderly man with a cheerful, ruddy face who, at first, seemed a little confused about their booking.

When Brad had confirmed that they only needed one

room he led them up a curved staircase to one of the surprisingly large turret rooms.

Loving it on sight, Joanne exclaimed, 'I've never stayed in a round room before!' Then curiously, 'Why did he think you'd asked for two rooms?'

'Because I had, originally. You see, I booked it on Saturday, shortly after we arrived at Lofoten. At that point I presumed we would need two.'

Trying not to blush, she said, 'Oh, I see…'

'Would you prefer a separate room?'

Going pink all the same, she shook her head.

'The good news is we have the only guest room in the house that has its own bathroom.'

Seeing he was waiting expectantly, she asked, 'What's the bad news?'

'That it's down a flight of stairs, and it has no shower.'

'I don't see either of those as being too much of a problem. Does it have a bath?'

'Oh, there's certainly a bath. Come and look.'

She following him through a small door, down a wooden staircase and into a bathroom the size of the bedroom.

As she stood admiring the huge bathtub that stood on gilded feet in the centre of the room, he gave her a glinting look from beneath thick, dark lashes. 'I don't know what you think, but in my opinion a bath might prove to be even more fun than a shower.'

'I'm sure you're right,' she agreed demurely.

He threw back his head and laughed joyously. 'A woman after my own heart! I'm convinced that if you've never made love in a Victorian bathtub, you haven't lived.

'Now, let's see, champagne hardly seems in keeping. What about a glass of mulled wine? Then later we'll go into town and I'll take you to a rather special restaurant for a birthday dinner.'

'It all sounds marvellous!'

'I hope it will be.'

*   *   *

Given the option of walking the half-mile or so down to town or being driven, the night being fine and clear, Joanne chose to walk.

'Don't forget it will be uphill on the way back,' Brad teased.

'Well, if I find I can't manage it, I'm sure you'll carry me,' she said insouciantly.

'Won't you be sorry if I use up all my strength?'

'I'm rather surprised you haven't already.'

He raised an eyebrow at her, leaving her covered in a glow of confusion.

The restaurant he had chosen was in the centre of the town, but on the far side of the river. Moonlight glinted on the fast-flowing water as it tumbled over smooth grey boulders, and the lamps on the embankment cast golden pools of light.

As they crossed the old cobbled bridge Brad pointed, and said, 'There it is, To Kokker. The name simply means two cooks. It's owned by twin brothers.'

To Joanne's surprise, the restaurant appeared to be nothing more than a large hut.

The inside did little to dispel that impression. Heated by an old black stove at either end, and lit by brass-bound oil lamps, it couldn't have been less pretentious.

Its dozen or so tables, most of which were full, were of scrubbed wood, the floor was sanded, and the crockery was thick and plain. But the welcome they received was a warm one, and the food, when it came, was out of this world.

They had pickled artichoke hearts followed by lobster in *beurre blanc* sauce, then *krumkake*, a wafer-thin shell of pastry filled with delicious blackberry cream.

Along with the excellent coffee, they were given a bottle of home-made dessert wine, which they shared with the brothers and the one remaining couple in the restaurant.

It developed into something of a party, and it was quite

late before they finally said their goodnights and left.

As hand in hand, like young lovers, they strolled across the bridge and headed out of town, he asked, 'Are you OK to walk? Or would you like me to carry you?'

'While it's a tempting offer, I think if you have any strength left I'd prefer you to keep it.'

'Practical as well as beautiful,' he said appreciatively.

At this time of night, apart from the odd car, there was very little traffic about, and even fewer pedestrians.

They had gone only fifty yards or so when the engine of a parked car roared into life. Dazzling headlights blinded them as the vehicle swerved onto the pavement and headed straight for them.

As Joanne stood momentarily paralysed Brad swept her off her feet, his impetus sending the pair of them sprawling into the safety of a narrow alleyway between two buildings. A split-second later the car careered harmlessly past, and went racing up the street.

Scrambling to his feet, Brad helped her up, asking urgently, 'Are you hurt in any way?'

'No, not a bit.' His arms had been around her, her body protected by his.

'Sure?'

'Quite sure. Are *you* all right?'

'Fine.'

'My lucky troll must be doing his stuff.'

She saw the glint of his smile in the gloom, before, setting her back against the wall, he said, 'Stay just where you are for a minute.'

'Why? Where are you going?'

'I just want to make sure they've gone.'

So he thought it had been deliberate. He thought whoever was responsible might possibly be back for a second try.

'I'm coming with you.'

'It might be safer if you waited here.'

She shook her head.

'Please, Joanne.'

'I've no intention of skulking in an alley while you go alone,' she said firmly.

'You're one stubborn woman,' he said. But he squeezed her hand.

As they emerged from the alleyway a car drew up with a rush and stopped by the kerb. Her heart in her mouth, Joanne recognised the people inside as the couple who had shared the wine in the restaurant.

The man jumped out and spoke to them in Norwegian. He seemed to be advocating a course of action Brad was reluctant to agree to.

After some further conversation, when Brad mentioned Trollfoss the man nodded and, apparently glad to be of help, opened the car's rear passenger door and ushered them inside.

When they were seated the woman turned her head and seemed to be asking anxiously if they were all right. By the time Brad had reassured her, they were drawing up outside the hotel.

He said, *'Tusen takk,'* while Joanne added her thanks in English. They clambered out and, repeating their thanks, stood for a moment to wave the pair off, before going inside.

Apart from a quick word with the desk clerk in the dimly lit lobby, Brad was silent until they reached their room.

It wasn't until he'd helped her off with her jacket and turned to hang it up that she got a proper look at him.

In the light from the red-shaded wall-lamps she saw his own jacket was torn and dirty, his left cheek was badly bruised and scraped, and trickles of blood had oozed down his face.

If he hadn't had his wits about him they might have both been killed or badly injured.

Reaction suddenly setting in, she turned icy cold, and, sinking down on one of the over-stuffed chairs, began to shake like a leaf.

Seeing her tremble, and taking in her pallor, he asked quickly, 'Are you certain you're all right?'

'Quite certain.' Through chattering teeth she added, 'But you've hurt your face.'

'It's just a graze,' he said dismissively.

'All the same it ought to be cleaned up. Do you think the hotel will have a first-aid box?'

'I'm sure they will. But I always carry an emergency kit.'

Having taken off his jacket and tossed it aside, he reached into his overnight bag and produced a small box. 'There should be everything necessary in there.'

Glad to have something positive to do, she got to her feet and, opening the lid, looked through the contents. 'These are just what we need.' Tearing open a pack of antiseptic wet-wipes, she instructed, 'Sit down there.'

He sat down like a lamb, his face the picture of innocence.

When she got near enough he threw his right arm around her waist and pulled her onto his knee. Then kissing the side of her neck, he remarked, 'I've always thought a nurse should get close to her patient.'

'Not that close,' she said severely.

But when she tried to wriggle free he merely held her tighter. 'Oh, very well,' she gave in, 'but turn your head that way…' A hand on his jaw, she pushed his face away.

When she had finished cleaning the wound she reached for a tube of ointment and put a thin smear over the raw area. 'There, that should do.'

'Thank you, Nurse. But you've forgotten something.'

'What have I forgotten?'

'When I was a very small boy and I hurt myself the nurse always used to kiss me better.'

'You're not a small boy any longer....'

'For which I'm truly thankful. My nurse had a moustache that prickled.'

Joanne was trying not to laugh, when he wheedled, 'Now I've told you my childhood secrets, what about that kiss?'

'All right. But just one.' She leaned forward to touch her lips to his good cheek.

'Call that a kiss?' he said contemptuously. '*This* is a kiss.' Growling and making horrendous slurping noises, he proceeded to demonstrate.

By the time he released her she was laughing helplessly, and the colour was back in her face.

'Feeling better?' he asked gently.

'Much better.'

And it was true. His fooling had lightened the atmosphere and allowed her to get her grip back.

Which was, she realised, why he'd done it.

CHAPTER TEN

'BRAD, I—'

A soft tap sounded through her words.

'This should be the coffee and brandy I ordered,' he said, and, pushing her gently into the chair he'd just vacated, headed for the door.

She heard the quiet murmur of voices, and a moment later he came back carrying a tray, which he set down on the bedside table.

Picking up the squat bottle, he poured a measure of the amber liquid into both glasses and handed her one. 'That should complete the cure.'

She took a cautious sip, coughed, and took another, feeling the brandy's fiery warmth dispel any lingering coldness.

When their glasses were empty he filled two coffee-cups and, sitting down on the edge of the bed, admitted soberly, 'I'm only sorry I ever involved you in all this.'

She shook her head. 'I'm not. Up till now my life has been sadly lacking in adventure.'

He saluted her spirit, before saying, 'Our friends, who left the restaurant shortly after we did and saw the whole thing, wanted to call the police.'

'Why didn't you let them?'

'It would have been a complete waste of time. With things happening so fast they didn't get the number of the car, and weren't sure of the colour, except that it was dark.

'In any case, the police would no doubt have regarded the incident simply as a drunken driver who had momentarily lost control.'

'And you're sure it wasn't?'

'Quite sure.'

'So this is part of the same trouble that brought you to Norway?'

'Very much a part. As I said, it's easier to deal with the opposition on home ground. Though not *too* close to home. It's my guess that it was planned to stage "the accident" well away from Bergen.

'I believe whoever was driving the car got to Lanadal ahead of us, and simply waited for the right opportunity. If we hadn't played into his hands by walking tonight I think he would have found some other way.'

'But who knew we were coming up to Lanadal?'

'Any number of people. You're probably the only one who didn't. I mentioned it to Erika when she asked me to go home with her. Helga, who packed our picnic basket, knew. So did the garage I hired the car from... Paul certainly did, and I've no doubt there were others.'

'I suppose you've still no idea who might be behind it all?'

'Having thought long and hard, I'm fairly sure I know. It's the only option that makes any real sense.'

'In that case, couldn't you go to the police?'

'It wouldn't do any good at this stage. I haven't any evidence as such, and this person is no common criminal. He's a rich and powerful man who most people would regard as being above suspicion.'

Puzzled, she asked, 'Have you any idea *why* he's doing it?'

'I believe there may be two connected reasons... The first is that his fleet of cargo vessels and the Dragon Shipping Line are in direct competition.

'The second, which sounds like the storyline to a soap opera, goes back over fifty years to when he and my grandfather were childhood friends.

'Both their families owned a shipping business, but as well as a lot of mountains Norway has a long coastline and a great deal of sea, so with more than enough space for them both to operate the two families never had a problem.

'Everything was fine until both young men happened to fall in love with, and want to marry, the same girl. They each proposed, and Grandfather won.

'Though later the other man married someone else, he and Grandfather ended up as lifelong rivals, not to say enemies, and he promised that one day, no matter how long it took, he'd find a way to even the score.

'When Grandfather died and I inherited the DSL he made me an offer for it, a very generous one, I might add, but it had been my grandfather's wish to keep the business in the family, so I refused to sell...

'He's made me two further offers since, both of which I've turned down.'

Frowning, Joanne asked, 'If, as you say, there's plenty of space for both shipping lines to operate, why does he want your company so badly?'

'He might well consider that a good way to even the score would be to take over and close down a business that Grandfather had spent a lifetime building up.'

Watching her expressive face, Brad added, 'While they're convincing-enough reasons for suspecting him, they're nowhere near good enough to enable me to make any firm accusations.'

'Yes, I see what you mean,' she said slowly. 'But if you can't find some way to stop him, presumably he'll go on with his campaign?'

'I think the answer to that is yes. Though it'll never get him what he wants.'

'Surely if he knows you he'll realise you won't bow to pressure?'

'Perhaps he doesn't know me that well. In any case I don't think he'll give up too easily. Beneath his outward respectability, he's a ruthless man. I believe he'll just try harder.'

She shivered. 'You don't mean to *kill* you?' Despite his grazed cheek, the whole thing seemed strangely unreal.

'I think he'd prefer *not* to have to go to those lengths. Tonight might just have been meant as a warning. A show of strength.

'On the other hand, if I didn't stand in his way and he only had Blake to deal with, he'd find the going a lot easier.

'As things stand at the moment, my cousin is next in line to inherit the Lancing empire.'

Sounding wearily cynical, he continued, 'Unfortunately, despite having a wife and two children, Blake makes a better playboy than a businessman. Which means he's always in need of money, and I couldn't trust him not to sell the DSL.

'Our competitor has probably checked him out and discovered as much.'

Horrified, she cried, 'But if that's the case, and he's as ruthless as you say…'

'It could well bump up the risk factor,' Brad admitted quietly.

'Even so, you've no intention of letting him have DSL?'

'Not the slightest! Would you?'

'No, I wouldn't.' Her answer was unequivocal. 'But there must be *something* you can do to stop him.'

'My best, maybe my only chance is to get some evidence that points directly to him. Faced with that, I hope and believe he'll back off. As a pillar of the church, and someone looked up to by the local community, he can't afford to lose his good reputation…

'Tomorrow when we get back to Bergen I'll talk to Paul and see if between us we can work out some sort of strategy.'

'Does Paul know his identity?'

Brad shook his head. 'Not yet. I was waiting to see if, off his own bat, he came up with anything that might corroborate my suspicions…

'But it's getting late and we've had more than enough of worries for one night… Would you like to use the bathroom first?'

When Joanne had washed her face and hands and cleaned her teeth she climbed the stairs back to the bedroom, and sank into the luxurious warmth and comfort of an old-fashioned goose-feather bed, while Brad took his turn in the bathroom.

Despite the upset the night had brought, and her anxiety over his safety, she was half-asleep by the time he returned.

As she lay watching him strip off his robe she noticed one arm seemed stiff, and when he turned she caught her breath. His left shoulder and arm, and his hip, were badly bruised.

'You told me you weren't hurt,' she said accusingly.

'I'm not.'

'What about all the bruising?'

Green eyes gleaming, he suggested, 'You could always try my favourite healing method.'

'I doubt if kissing will do much good.'

'Well, at the very least it'll take my mind off it.'

Next morning they woke to another fine, sunny day, and after a late-ish breakfast made a visit to the Troll Falls, which were spectacular, before starting back to Bergen.

Though Brad appeared to be relaxed and carefree, she knew by his frequent glances in the rear-view mirror and the caution with which he drove that he was on his guard.

Early afternoon they stopped for a meal at a roadside restaurant that smelt of sun-warmed wood and pine-resin.

'Would you like to eat indoors or out?' Brad asked.

'Oh, alfresco, I think.'

Out front was a wooden deck with tubs of bright flowers, and small tables covered with red-checked cloths. From it, there was a good view of the dusty road winding down the mountainside in a spectacular series of horseshoe bends.

While they sat enjoying the sunshine and waiting for their food he said, 'If you'll excuse me, I must phone Paul.'

'Of course.'

When Paul answered Brad told him crisply, 'We'll be back in Bergen by late afternoon, and I'd like to talk to you... Yes, that might be best... You have...?' Then sharply, 'You're not hurt...? Well, take care. See you then.'

As he dropped the phone back into his pocket she asked anxiously, 'Is Paul all right?'

'Yes, thank God. He was on one of our wharfs last night checking out a report of an intruder, when a piece of heavy lifting equipment came adrift and missed him by inches.'

This latest news made the threat to Brad's life seem all the more urgent, more *real*, and she shivered. If anything happened to him...

Watching all the colour drain from her face, he said, 'There's really no need to worry. Paul assured me he'd escaped without a scratch.' Then sardonically, 'I hope this extreme reaction doesn't mean you've fallen for him?'

'Of course I haven't fallen for him.'

'That's just as well. He's carrying a torch for Erika.'

'Yes, I know. He told me.'

Brad raised a dark brow. 'Paul's not usually given to personal confidences.' An edge to his voice, he added, 'You two must have found an instant rapport?'

Steadily, she agreed, 'I suppose we did.'

'Is that why, thinking I was going off with Erika, you immediately decided to ask him to take you home?'

'I didn't *immediately decide* anything of the kind,' Joanne told him. 'My first thought was to get a taxi, but Mr Reiersen said, owing to the amount of functions taking place, most taxi firms would be fully booked.

'He suggested that, as Paul had come in his own car, and

was living quite close to Lofoten, *he* would no doubt be pleased to take me.

'I thought Paul's car was off the road, but—'

'Did you mention that to Reiersen?'

'I'm afraid so. Though I didn't tell him *why*.'

'What did he say?'

Joanne's recollection was good, and she was able to answer, 'He said, "There was a spot of trouble with his brakes, I gather, but obviously he's had them fixed."'

'Did he say anything else?'

'Yes, he added, "Randall isn't the kind of young man to let grass grow under his feet. If he wasn't working for Brad *I* wouldn't mind employing him. It didn't take him long to get on to Mussen..."'

She stopped speaking as a waiter brought a colourful dish of meatballs in tomato sauce, on a bed of green fettucini.

When they had been served, his face oddly tense, Brad asked, 'You're sure he said Mussen?'

'Quite sure. The name seemed to ring a bell, but I couldn't think why...'

'I presume Reiersen was not altogether sober?'

'No. Before he asked me to dance, Paul warned me that he'd been drinking.'

Brad frowned. 'I hope it wasn't too much of an ordeal?'

Remembering how shaken she'd felt, she said, 'No, of course not.'

'The lies fairly hop out of you.'

'All right, it wasn't very pleasant. But there's no harm done.'

His face relaxing, Brad squeezed her hand. 'I think you'll find an awful lot of good will come out of it.'

By the time they reached Lofoten it was early evening and dusk was starting to cover the bright day with cobwebby veils of lilac and blue.

Brad stopped the car by the main entrance and, carrying their bags and the picnic basket, ushered Joanne inside.

Paul was sitting in front of the stove in the deserted foyer, waiting for them. Watching them cross to the desk, he raised a hand in salute.

When Brad had returned the picnic basket with a word of thanks Helga said, 'I hope all went well?'

'Very well.'

'I will get Edvard to take up your bags.'

'And perhaps you can manage a pot of tea?'

'Of course.'

'Enjoy your birthday trip?' Paul asked cheerfully as they joined him.

'Very much,' Joanne answered.

'Though we did have a spot of bother in Lanadal,' Brad said, and proceeded to explain briefly what had happened.

Paul whistled through his teeth. 'Could have been nasty... And it ties in with the report I had back from the garage. There's no doubt that the car's braking system had been deliberately tampered with... Which seems to suggest that we're all targets.'

'It also suggests that it's high time we did something about it.'

'What *can* we do?' Paul asked gloomily.

'Now, I might just be able to answer that...' Brad broke off as their tray of tea arrived.

'Shall I pour?' Joanne offered.

Paul grinned. 'Thanks, Joanne.'

She had just started to pour, when a voice said sarcastically, 'My, but isn't this cosy?'

Beautifully made-up and dressed in a glacier-blue costume that matched her eyes, Erika was watching them in a derisory fashion.

Her gleaming silvery-blonde hair falling straight to her shoulders, her flawless skin pale, she looked like some exquisite ice maiden, totally out of place in the golden warmth of the foyer.

The two men rose to their feet.

'Won't you join us?' Brad asked politely.

'I wanted a word in private.'

'Tell you what,' Paul suggested to Joanne, 'shall we take a walk and—?'

'There's really no need,' Brad said firmly. 'I'm sure that whatever Erika has to say can be said in front of you both.'

Looking furious, Erika said, 'Very well. If that's how you want it.'

Then, addressing Joanne, 'I have something of yours. You left it at the party.' From her own handbag she produced the small silver evening purse.

'Thank you.' Joanne held out her hand.

Making no attempt to hand the purse over, the blonde went on, 'I must say, I'm surprised you went without it. But I suppose when you realised you'd left it you dared not kick up a fuss in case Brad found out what you'd been up to.'

'I'm afraid I don't know what you're talking about,' Joanne said flatly.

'I might have expected you to act the innocent.'

'Perhaps you could come to the point?' Brad suggested.

'The point is, your *secretary* has been selling information. When, having heard some odd rumours, Daddy casually asked her how things were with the DSL, she hinted that her answer should be worth money...

'He was shocked, but clearly *someone* took her up on the offer.'

'What utter rubbish,' Joanne exclaimed.

'Then how do you account for the money?'

'What money?'

'Would you mind telling me what's going on?' Brad demanded.

'If you want to know what's going on, I suggest you look inside this bag.' Erika thrust the purse into his hand.

His voice icy, Brad informed her, 'I've no intention of looking in Miss Winslow's purse.'

'Don't be a fool!' Erika snatched back the purse, and opening it, turned it upside-down. Onto the table fell a comb, a small compact, a tube of lipstick, a couple of tissues, and a thick wad of kroner.

As Joanne stared blankly at the money Erika said with unconcealed triumph, 'There! What did I tell you? While she was dancing the common little tart was obviously selling—'

'That's quite enough!' Though quiet, Brad's voice cracked like a whip. 'I'm sure Miss Winslow was doing nothing of the kind.'

'Instead of trying to defend her, why don't you ask her how the money got there?'

Her temper rising, Joanne said, 'I haven't the faintest idea. Unless you or your father put it there.'

'How dare you suggest such a thing?'

Catching Erika's eye, Paul asked mildly, 'May I say something?'

Darting an angry look at Brad, Erika said, 'It would be nice to hear from someone who isn't biased.'

'I'm glad you agree I'm not biased, because I'm in a good position to give you the facts.

'You see, I was with Miss Winslow for most of the evening, and when I wasn't actually *with* her I was keeping an eye on her, as Brad had asked me to—'

'There you are—' Erika began.

'I don't mean for any reason other than she knew no one there, and Brad wasn't expecting her to be made particularly welcome.

'Now, I can tell you categorically that, apart from myself the only people Miss Winslow danced with were Brad and

our father. I certainly didn't give her the money, and I
really can't imagine Brad did…'

'I hope you're not accusing—'

'I'm not *accusing* your father of anything.'

'That's just as well. You can take it from me, Daddy
ever *touched* her purse.'

Paul shook his head. 'I happened to see him put it on a
side-table.'

'When was that?' Brad asked sharply.

Her face paper-white, Joanne explained, 'It was when Mr
Reiersen asked me to dance. I dropped the purse and he
picked it up. When I remarked that it was a bit of a nuisance, he disposed of it for me. I'm afraid I'd forgotten all
about it…'

Gathering up the purse and the items that went with it,
Brad turned to Paul and said abruptly, 'Perhaps you'll be
good enough to see Erika to her car?'

'Of course. How long before you want me back?'

'Fifteen minutes.'

'Fifteen minutes it is.'

Without another word, Brad took Joanne's arm and hurried her upstairs.

When they reached their suite he tossed the purse and
the rest of the things onto the table, and pushed her gently
into a chair. 'Do you feel up to telling me exactly what
Reiersen said about the DSL?'

'He said he'd heard a whisper that there'd been more
trouble, including a fire in one of the hotels. He wanted to
know what you were doing about it, if you were considering calling in the police.

'When I told him I didn't know he said perhaps I needed
time to think about it, and that useful information could
pay big dividends…I told Paul all about it.'

'Take your time, and if you can remember I'd like the
whole conversation verbatim.' Brad's voice held sup-
pressed excitement.

As closely as she could, Joanne repeated what had been said word for word, stumbling a little over the more personal parts like, 'There's such a thing as misplaced loyalty and once Brad's had his fun...' but leaving nothing out.

'He'd just offered to show me round the new leisure complex he'd built, and mentioned some wonderful shop in the arcade when Paul rescued me.'

Looking furious, Brad muttered, 'I'd like to break his damn neck.'

'It's all right—' she began awkwardly.

'But it *isn't* all right.' He took her cold hand. 'I'm sorry. The whole thing is my fault. I should never have put you in a position where you could be insulted like that.

'If he hadn't had too much to drink he would no doubt have been a great deal more cautious about what he said...

'When he sobered up he must have realised he'd made a mistake approaching you in that way.

'Presumably, afraid you'd tell me, he thought up this scheme to turn the tables and try to discredit you—'

A knock at the door made him release her hand and call, 'Come in.'

'All sorted out?' Paul asked. At Brad's nod, he went on, 'I've been wondering about Reiersen for some time now. When Joanne told me he'd tried to bribe her I made up my mind to talk to you about it. Now this money seems to clinch things.'

'You don't think it might have been Erika's doing?'

'I did wonder about that. I must admit that I wouldn't put it past her.

'But when I asked her how she came by the purse she said one of the servants had brought it to her, and she thought she recognised it as Joanne's.

'She swears that when she looked inside the money was already there. I think I believe her.'

'And I'm inclined to think you're right.'

'So *you* believe Reiersen's behind everything?'

'I've thought so for a little while. The problem was getting some evidence. Now, thanks to Joanne's memory for conversations, we may be able to find something that leads directly back to him.'

Picking up the wad of money, Brad thrust it into his pocket.

'You're going to tackle Reiersen now?'

'Yes, but first I want to call on Mussen.'

'You want me with you?'

'No. I'd like you to keep Joanne company.'

Everything falling into place to make a far from pleasant picture, she said quickly, 'I don't need anyone to keep me company. It would make more sense to take Paul with you.'

'I think Joanne's right,' Paul urged.

Seeing by the look on Brad's face that they were both wasting their breath, she promised, 'If it makes you feel any happier, I'll bolt the door and I won't set foot out of the suite.'

'You may need a witness to what's said,' Paul pointed out practically.

Apparently seeing the sense of that, Brad agreed, 'Very well.'

As Joanne breathed a sigh of relief he reminded her, 'Don't forget to bolt the door as soon as we've gone.'

'I won't.'

He clapped Paul on the shoulder. 'Come along, then. While we go I'll fill in the gaps.'

Despite the music-centre and the well-stocked bookcases, Joanne found herself unable to settle to anything.

For a while she pottered about, changing the water in the flowers Brad had given her, washing out her stockings and hanging them over the towel-rail, taking a shower...

And all the time *waiting*.

It seemed an age before she heard a rap at the door and

Brad's voice calling her name. A glance at the clock showed it was under two hours since he had left.

Hurrying to let him in, she asked eagerly, 'Is everything all right?'

'Thanks to you, everything is fine.'

Relief turning her knees to water, she sank down on the couch. 'I'm so *glad*, though I'm sure it isn't thanks to me.'

Taking a seat beside her, Brad disagreed, 'That's just where you're wrong. If you hadn't remembered Reiersen mentioning Mussen...'

'Though the name rang a bell, I'm still not sure...'

'As we were walking back from Bryggen, if you recall, I told you how Paul set a trap and caught a cargo-handler named Mussen... The man admitted bearing a grudge because his brother had been sacked for stealing...'

'Of course... I'm afraid at the time I was only half listening...'

'Perhaps your mind was on other things,' Brad suggested smoothly.

Remembering just what *had* been occupying her mind, she felt the colour rise in her cheeks. 'So what happened when you went to see him?' she asked hurriedly.

'We had a talk, and he admitted that a man named Andersen had suggested the way to work off his grudge, and had actually paid him.'

Seeing Joanne was looking a little blank, he explained, *'Andersen is one of Reiersen's top men.'*

'I see!' she breathed.

'After Mussen was caught, knowing he'd been a fool, and grateful that both he and his brother had been allowed to keep their jobs, he told Andersen to get someone else to do his dirty work.

'When I laid my cards on the table, and Mussen realised how serious things were getting, he gave me the names of a couple of men he felt sure were now working for Andersen.

'Armed with that information, and having decided to try a little bluff, Paul and I went to see Reiersen. First I gave him back his money, then, without involving Mussen, named a few names and told him that if the attacks didn't stop immediately and for good we had a complete dossier ready to put before the police. Faced with the threat of being exposed, he backed off, as I'd guessed he would.'

'You mean he *admitted* he was behind it?'

'No, he's too clever for that. He simply said he was sure we'd have no further trouble.

'Then he asked me if I wouldn't reconsider the offer he'd made the night of the party... Remember I told you we were talking business...?'

Joanne nodded.

'Well, in a nutshell, his offer was this, that our two business empires should merge, and that I should marry Erika and stay in Norway to run both of them.

'He said, "It's time there was a younger man at the helm. If I'd had a son I would have handed over the reins sooner. I'm nearly seventy-four now. When I'm gone you can have complete control."'

Her throat dry, Joanne managed, 'He said *reconsider*, so presumably you turned him down the first time?'

'Yes. I think the car incident in Lanadal was his response to that refusal.

'Tonight, in Paul's presence, he offered me complete control as soon as Erika and I had our first child. He said, "If you agree, one day your son, and my grandson, will take over a vast empire...

'"This time I hope you'll say yes. It's what Erika wants you to do."'

Feeling as though she was bleeding to death, Joanne asked though dry lips, 'So you agreed?'

He raised a dark brow. 'Have you ever noticed me doing what Erika wants me to do?'

'No… But it's obvious that she's in love with you, and—'

'Erika is a spoilt child who *thinks* she's in love with me. And before you ask, I've given her no encouragement to think that.'

'Oh… So what did you say?'

'I refused, of course. I told him politely that, having lodged the "dossier" with my bank, I intended to leave Paul in Norway to run DSL for me.'

'Paul won't mind?'

'No, he loves Norway, and he's still prepared to take his chance with Erika. Once I'm out of the picture, he may well succeed.

'For both their sakes I hope so… Though I would certainly class that marriage as a "noble daring".'

Filled with joy, she asked, 'So what will you do? Stay on for the holiday you were talking about?'

'I'm not sure,' he said abruptly. 'I may take a day or two to think about it. In the meantime I'll book you on the first plane back to London…'

Shock drained the joy away.

So it was over.

'I should never have forced you to come to Norway in the first place. Never made you wear that dress.'

'It's a lovely dress. And at least some good came out of it.'

But as though she hadn't spoken he went on, 'I've made so many mistakes, and all because I was furious at being misjudged… If you'd checked your "facts" you would have found that it was Blake who has the bad reputation. I don't know why his wife stays with him.'

'Perhaps she loves him.'

'If she does, he doesn't deserve it.'

'Brad…I-I'm sorry I misjudged you… If it hadn't been for what happened while we were having dinner that night, and then later on in the taxi…' Her words tailed off.

He sighed. 'When it became obvious what you were up to I decided to play along. I wanted to frighten you, to teach you a lesson.

'I've never had any designs on your sister. To be brutally honest, she's not my type. When I told you I'd never treated her as anything other than a good secretary, it was perfectly true.

'It's also true that I didn't know she was married. She started work as Miss Winslow and she never reported any change of status. If you don't believe me you can check with Personnel.'

'I do believe you,' Joanne said. 'Though with so much going on at the time it scarcely registered that Paul wasn't aware that she was married. He remarked that he'd always known her as Miss Winslow.'

'Well, I'm glad you have some kind of proof.'

'I don't need any proof. While I've been trying to tell myself you were the womaniser I first thought you, I knew in my heart you were nothing of the kind.

'Every single thing you've done or said has gone to prove the opposite.'

'Apart from the fact that you were a virgin when you came, and now you're not.'

'That was my choice,' she said firmly, 'and, as I told you, I don't regret it. Though I do regret listening to Milly. I'm sure that, fancying herself in love with you, she saw things as she *wanted* them to be...

'When you said Milly was merely your secretary I should have believed you. The mistakes that have been made are all mine.'

He shook his head. 'I've made my share, that's why I don't intend to make any more.'

Desperately wanting just a few more weeks of happiness, she pleaded, 'You don't think sending me back to London might be a mistake? You said you wanted companionship, someone to share things with... If you don't love Erika...couldn't I...?'

'You're not the kind to have affairs.'

'Oh, I don't know... I'm enjoying my first.'

'I don't happen to want to carry on having an affair with you,' he said flatly.

Ashamed that she'd thrown herself at him, she flushed scarlet.

Taking her hot face between his palms, he said, 'If you intend to stay, it'll have to be on my terms.'

'What are your terms?' she asked unsteadily.

'I want you to marry me.'

Unable to believe it, she shook her head. 'You can't want to marry me.'

'This isn't some sudden decision,' he told her. 'I've been waiting all my life for a wife who looks like you, and enjoys life the way you do, and laughs at the same things that make me laugh, and eats like a navvy, and kisses me back as though she loves me, even if she doesn't—'

'Oh, but I do.'

'I'm glad about that. If you'd simply gone back to London I don't know what I would have done. But I had to give you the chance.

'Do you want to be married in Norway? Or would you like to wait until we return to England?'

'I'd love to be married in Norway.'

'In Norway women tend to wear their wedding rings on the right hand, but if that bothers you I'll buy you one for each.

'And, speaking of rings, first thing tomorrow I'd like you to send Trevor's ring back and break the news to your family.'

A faint cloud appearing on the horizon, Joanne said worriedly, 'It's OK. I've already broken things off with Trevor; I rang him at the airport, when I realised I wanted to be with you. I don't know what Milly will think...'

'As you've told me repeatedly, your sister is a married woman. She's made her choice, and you are entitled to make yours. So does it really matter what Milly thinks?'

The cloud lifted. 'No, I suppose it doesn't.'

'There, now, everything's settled, so before I take you out to dinner, come and shower with me…'

Mischievously she said, 'I had a shower while I was waiting for you to come back.'

'I thought you agreed with the sentiment "Gather ye rosebuds while ye may".'

'Do you know, you're the only man I've ever known who can quote Herrick?'

He leered at her. 'I have other, more exciting talents that are best put to use in the shower.'

She pretended to consider. 'Well, I suppose I could always enjoy another.'

'I'll make sure you do.'

He took her hand and led her into the bedroom.

Propped on the bedside table, alongside the flowers he'd given her, was her birthday card.

'Now I'm going to marry you, you could at least tell me what my card says.'

He grinned at her, his green eyes gleaming through thick, sooty lashes.

'Well, I suppose it's appropriate now. It says, "A happy birthday to my very own deer." And my personal message reads, *"PS I love you."'*

Modern Romance™
...seduction and
passion guaranteed

Tender Romance™
...love affairs that
last a lifetime

Sensual Romance™
...sassy, sexy and
seductive

Blaze
...sultry days and
steamy nights

Medical Romance™
...medical drama on
the pulse

Historical Romance™
...rich, vivid and
passionate

27 new titles every month.

*With all kinds of Romance for
every kind of mood...*

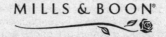

MILLS & BOON

CHRISTMAS
SECRETS

Three Festive Romances

CAROLE MORTIMER   CATHERINE SPENCER
DIANA HAMILTON

Available from 15th November 2002

Available at most branches of WH Smith,
Tesco, Martins, Borders, Eason, Sainsbury's
and all good paperback bookshops.

1202/59/MB50

FREE!

2 Books
and a surprise gift!

We would like to take this opportunity to thank you for reading this Mills & Boon® book by offering you the chance to take TWO more specially selected titles from the Modern Romance™ series absolutely FREE! We're also making this offer to introduce you to the benefits of the Reader Service™—

- ★ FREE home delivery
- ★ FREE gifts and competitions
- ★ FREE monthly Newsletter
- ★ Books available before they're in the shops
- ★ Exclusive Reader Service discount

Accepting these FREE books and gift places you under no obligation to buy; you may cancel at any time, even after receiving your free shipment. Simply complete your details below and return the entire page to the address below. *You don't even need a stamp!*

YES! Please send me 2 free Modern Romance books and a surprise gift. I understand that unless you hear from me, I will receive 4 superb new titles every month for just £2.55 each, postage and packing free. I am under no obligation to purchase any books and may cancel my subscription at any time. The free books and gift will be mine to keep in any case.

P2ZEB

Ms/Mrs/Miss/Mr ....Initials............................

BLOCK CAPITALS PLEASE

Surname..

Address..

....

....Postcode ....

Send this whole page to:
UK: The Reader Service, FREEPOST CN81, Croydon, CR9 3WZ
EIRE: The Reader Service, PO Box 4546, Kilcock, County Kildare (stamp required)